They wanted a
they must fight

Jordan flung her door open and jumped from the jeep. As Ellie crouched to follow, Jordan leaned close to her ear and whispered, "Bring your bag and hurry."

Propelling Ellie to the outhouse beside the cafe, Jordan opened the door and pushed her inside.

"Ouch! Don't be so rough. You know I bruise easily."

"Ellie, sober up and listen to me. Our guide's packing—"

"Yes, I noticed he has a nice package." Ellie smirked then belched.

Jordan grabbed Ellie by her upper arms and shook her hard, itching to slap her friend across the face. "Pay attention—our lives may depend on it! He has a concealed dagger, a roll of duct tape on the floor of the Jeep, and a tattoo with 'Madras 16' on his upper arm. I recognized the tattoo from last night's news. He's a gang member and some of his buddies were arrested for drug trafficking in La Ceiba."

Frustrated with the still-vacant look in Ellie's eyes, Jordan gave her another shake before repeating, "La Ceiba. You know. The place where the airport bus let us off."

Ellie's liquor-fueled high crashed and burned. "Holy shit. You got to be kidding!"

"Do I look like I'm kidding? Follow me."

What could be better than a week of sipping mojitos, basking in the sun, and listening to waves lap against a Caribbean beach? Nothing, according to Jordan Blair and her friend, Ellie Cassidy.

Until their vacation takes a sinister turn...

The former occupant of their room has vanished and the resort manager is unconcerned. He suggests the woman has taken off for a romantic interlude with a sailboat skipper. Given the visible police presence, Jordan doesn't buy it. Another guest attaches himself to Jordan and Ellie, but his covert activities arouse Jordan's suspicions. Could he have been involved with the woman's disappearance?

Plagued by unanswered questions, Jordan trusts the wrong man. Now, she and Ellie are running for their lives. Will her survival skills save them or result in a fight she can't win?

KUDOS for *Targeted*

In *Targeted* by Donna Warner and Gloria Ferris, Jordan Blair is a Canadian cop on vacation in the Caribbean with her friend Ellie Cassidy. They wanted to soak up some sun, have a few umbrella drinks, and maybe meet some hot guys. What they didn't expect is to get embroiled in a missing tourist and other dangerous shenanigans. Upon their arrival at the resort, they discover that their room's last occupant turned up missing and no one seems to care. Is it just the devil-may-care attitude so prevalent in the Caribbean world, or does someone have something to hide? Could it be the charming resort manager? Or perhaps the mysterious male guest who joins them for dinner and isn't quite what he seems? The story is very well written with charming, engaging characters and a plot that is full of surprises. It's short enough to read in a single sitting, but so much fun, you'll want to read it again and again. ~ *Taylor Jones, Reviewer*

Targeted by Donna Warner and Gloria Ferris is a mystery/detective/suspense/thriller with interesting characters in a romantic setting. Our heroines, Jordan and Ellie, make a good pair, with Ellie's quasi-cluelessness a nice counterpart to Canadian cop Jordan's sharp eye and quick brain. Taking a vacation together in the Caribbean, the two friends arrive at their resort and immediately run into trouble. First the suitcase delivered to their room that's supposed to be Ellie's, isn't. Hers has apparently been lost by the airlines, and the one that showed up actually belongs to the woman who last stayed in their room, and who since has disappeared. Not that anyone seems to notice. Or care. The resort manager, Tate, just shrugs and says she probably ran off for a romantic getaway with a local. But Jordan isn't so sure. As she begins to investigate, she uncovers much more than she wanted to, especially when she supposed to be on vacation. *Targeted*, aside from being quite well written, has a slew of fascinating and realistic characters, an exotic setting, and a strong plot. Combined with the vivid descriptions, fast-paced action, intriguing mystery, and flashes of off-beat humor, it makes for a great read. ~ *Regan Murphy, Reviewer*

ACKNOWLEDGEMENTS

Much gratitude to novelist, Dr. D. L. Houghton who critiqued *Targeted*'s many drafts and provided valuable input. And our thanks to beta readers Lara Inneo and Alyssa MacPherson whose insightful comments were extremely helpful.

TARGETED

Donna Warner
and
Gloria Ferris

A Black Opal Books Publication

GENRE: MYSTERY/SUSPENSE/WOMEN SLEUTHS

This is a work of fiction. Names, places, characters and incidents are either the product of the author's imagination or are used fictitiously, and any resemblance to any actual persons, living or dead, businesses, organizations, events or locales is entirely coincidental. All trademarks, service marks, registered trademarks, and registered service marks are the property of their respective owners and are used herein for identification purposes only. The publisher does not have any control over or assume any responsibility for author or third-party websites or their contents.

TARGETED
Copyright © 2015 by Donna Warner & Gloria Ferris
Cover Design by Jackson Cover Designs
All cover art copyright © 2015
All Rights Reserved
Print ISBN: 978-1-626943-50-6

First Publication: NOVEMBER 2015

All rights reserved under the International and Pan-American Copyright Conventions. No part of this book may be reproduced or transmitted in any form or by any means, electronic or mechanical, including photocopying, recording, or by any information storage and retrieval system, without permission in writing from the publisher.

WARNING: The unauthorized reproduction or distribution of this copyrighted work is illegal. Criminal copyright infringement, including infringement without monetary gain, is investigated by the FBI and is punishable by up to 5 years in federal prison and a fine of $250,000. Anyone pirating our ebooks will be prosecuted to the fullest extent of the law and may be liable for each individual download resulting therefrom.

ABOUT THE PRINT VERSION: If you purchased a print version of this book without a cover, you should be aware that the book is stolen property. It was reported as "unsold and destroyed" to the publisher, and neither the author nor the publisher has received any payment for this "stripped book."

IF YOU FIND AN EBOOK OR PRINT VERSION OF THIS BOOK BEING SOLD OR SHARED ILLEGALLY, PLEASE REPORT IT TO: lpn@blackopalbooks.com

Published by Black Opal Books **http://www.blackopalbooks.com**

DEDICATION

We dedicate this book to our grandchildren.
We hope we'll be around when you're old enough to read it
so we can defend our twisted and
occasionally frightening prose.

CHAPTER 1

A hand pushed aside the blossoms of a red ginger shrub and aimed high-powered binoculars at La Ceiba beach. It was the perfect spot. Close enough to watch and listen, yet far enough away to avoid being detected.

Tourists spilled from the sweltering airport buses. Excited voices carried snippets of conversations about their impending arrival at one of the most exclusive holiday destinations in Honduras—the Barefoot Bay resort on Roatán Island.

A young woman with dark hair bunched into a ponytail and long, bare legs jumped from the top step of the bus. She dropped her tote and waited for her companion to descend.

The second woman was petite and curvaceous, with hair the color of fire. Her ivory skin appeared luminous under the bright sun. They wound their way through a knot of fellow travelers to stand under the spotty shade of a palm tree.

The watcher with the binoculars tracked their movements.

Shouts from the bus driver dragged the women's attention from the magnificent view of the Caribbean Sea. They watched with amusement as the driver hollered and signalled until he captured the attention of two Honduran teens sitting on an idling ATV hitched to a cart. The boys drove over and dismounted at the open luggage bay. With a noticeable lack of enthusiasm, they began tossing suitcases. Some hit the cart, others landed with a thud on the hot, white sand.

The brunette turned to her friend. "Look on the bright side, Ellie. At least your luggage won't be dented."

"Very funny, Jordan. I can't believe the airline lost my frigging luggage." Ellie dropped her bag to unfasten the lower buttons on her filmy yellow blouse. Grabbing the bottom ends, she savagely twisted the material into a knot.

Jordan patted her arm. "I'm sure it will turn up before the day is over. Meanwhile, my clothes are yours."

"Thanks. Good thing I have my bikini, a couple of pairs of thongs, and my toothbrush in my carry on."

"That's all you'll need, my friend."

TARGETED 3

The binoculars lingered on the swell of fabric above the red head's bare midriff.

The driver slammed the luggage bin and shouted to the anxious tourists, "*Señoras y señores*, you must wait there for the ferry boat to Roatán." He pointed a stubby, nicotine-stained finger toward the dock. "It should be here in *quince minutos*."

"What did he say?" Ellie asked as she picked up her tote.

A fellow traveller, standing nearby, overheard the question. He strolled over to Ellie.

The binoculars swivelled to the male intruder.

"The chap said the ferry would be here in fifteen minutes." The man's lopsided smile magically transformed Ellie's funk over her lost luggage to awareness of an attractive male.

"I'm Darcy Piermont." There was muscle under the man's expensive clothes. Tattoos snaked along his forearms and calves. He had rugged, clean-shaven features and his blond hair was short on the back and sides, while the top was two inches longer and gelled into a short, spikey mohawk.

Ellie smiled widely and moved closer to the man, while Jordan simply nodded a greeting.

Fingers tightened on the binoculars. A flash of sunlight reflected off the lenses as they slowly withdrew. The scarlet blossoms shuddered then fell back into place.

CHAPTER 2

Darcy extended his hand to both women in turn. "I spend a lot of time in Spain. I'm at your service for any translation needs." He spoke to both women, but his eyes found Jordan's and sought to hold the connection.

Jordan broke eye contact, pretending an interest in a soaring cormorant diving for its lunch.

Her friend stepped in to fill the awkward silence. "It's a pleasure to meet you, Darcy. I'm Ellie Cassidy and this is Jordan Blair. I couldn't help noticing your awesome tattoos."

Darcy's lips upturned in a half smile. "These are strictly for advertising. I assure you the rest of my body is unspoiled. Or at least ink-free."

He winked at Jordan when she glanced back at him.

Ellie giggled and nudged his shoulder. "I have a couple of tats as well. But I'll need to get to know you better before unveiling them."

They weren't even on the island yet and, already, her friend had her eye on a playmate. Hoping to steer the conversation back to less intimate territory, Jordan asked, "So, Darcy, are you a tattoo artist like Ed Hardy?"

"No, love. I'm seldom sober enough to hold a needle, let alone draw with one. I own an interest in a tattoo parlor in Montreal along with a couple of businesses abroad."

A self-confessed drunk and a wealthy playboy? Red flags of caution unfurled in Jordan's mind.

"My, you are a man of mystery, aren't you?" Ellie cooed, fluttering her sea green eyes up at Darcy. "It's cool to meet a fellow Canadian. Are you staying at Barefoot Bay resort, too?"

"*Oui*, I am." Darcy pulled Armani sunglasses from his travel bag and slipped them over his bloodshot blue eyes.

"Let's hook up later for drinks," Ellie encouraged. "You can tell us what each of your tattoos represents."

"With pleasure, c*hérie*."

As they approached the beach, Jordan worked at being more cordial. "Does managing your businesses require extensive travel?"

"Yes, but I enjoy it. I've puked my way around the globe once or twice."

Ellie guffawed and slapped Darcy on the back.

Jordan managed not to roll her eyes.

"Darcy, do you know how long it will take the ferry to get us to Roatán Island?" Ellie asked.

"About seventy-five minutes. The *Galaxy Wave* is a powerhouse of a vessel. *Bon*—here she comes now."

The mammoth ferry taxied to the dock with the grace of a swimming swan. Two crew members dropped a wooden plank and beckoned the travelers to board.

Jordan glanced back at the bus as two armed cops in khaki uniforms motioned for their driver to leave. When the bus pulled away, the stern-looking men strode toward the ferry and butted to the front of the line. No one objected.

Following Jordan's gaze, Darcy explained, "That's the local *policía*."

"It's strange to see police carrying rifles instead of having holstered handguns."

"Yes, well, you'll find a lot of differences in policing practices between Honduras and Canada, my pet. It would blow your mind to see the conditions of the local jail. It services a population from three islands. Prisoners have to rely on family or friends, if they have any, to bring them food."

"That seems rather harsh," Jordan said. "In Canadian prisons, inmates complain if they're denied Internet privileges."

"Some of the inmates here would rob you blind and cut your throat without a second thought. Honduras has the highest murder rate per capita in the world. So don't wander away from the resort unless you're with a group." He motioned for them to join the boarding queue. "Shall we?"

An expression of concern crossed Ellie's face for a brief moment. Then she tossed her thick mane, linked her arm in Darcy's, and smiled up at him.

Jordan's hand automatically reached to her side where her weapon usually hung from her equipment belt. Feeling sheepish, she scanned the beach before following behind Darcy and Ellie.

CHAPTER 3

Jordan craned her neck to see to the front of the line. Why were they boarding at a snail's pace? "They're making everyone go through a metal detector?"

"Neat, maybe they'll do a strip search, too," Ellie said, breaking into a fit of giggles when she saw Jordan's warning glance.

"As I alluded to earlier—" Darcy paused for effect. "Precautions like this are necessary in the Caribbean. Crime is high and murders are bad for the tourist trade. Not to mention the tourists."

Stepping aboard, Jordan faced two officers who took their work very seriously.

"Arms up," the younger officer demanded.

Jordan felt like she was back in kindergarten, playing

Simon Says. He ran a hand-held wand along her arms and down the sides of her body. Since it was obvious she didn't have a weapon hidden in her sleeveless top, Jordan considered this exercise overkill but had no choice but to comply.

಄಄

The trio ignored the inside cabin and settled themselves on port side benches to enjoy the bright sunshine and salty ocean spray. Conversations were drowned out after the ferry backed up and sped out to sea. Waves dashed by at a dizzying pace as the craft flew past the islands of Utila and Cayos Cochinos. Suddenly, the throttle was pulled back and static emitted from speakers.

"*Hola.* I am Captain Alvero. We are now in International waters, so it's party time! Free drinks inside at the cabin bar."

After the applause subsided, island dance music exploded from the speakers. Once the line cleared, Darcy got up and made a beeline to the bar. He called back to Ellie, "Save me a dance. I'll get our drinks."

The *Galaxy Wave* gained speed again, making it a challenge for dancing passengers to avoid wearing their rum punch drinks.

Ellie pivoted to face Jordan. "It was worth living on Kraft dinners and curbing shopping trips over the winter to save for this trip."

TARGETED

Laughing and struggling to pull windswept hair from her mouth, Jordan yelled back, "You got that right."

As the ferry transported them to their destination, they danced to the heady beat of the Beach Boys' "Kokomo." A week of relaxation and fun lured them like an addictive drug.

CHAPTER 4

Jordan leaned her five-foot-eight-inch frame against the ferry's railing as it taxied to Barefoot Bay's long dock. After the crew secured the vessel and dropped the plank, Darcy stepped off and extended a hand to each of the women.

Jordan looked past him to the stunning beauty of the boutique resort. Nestled on four acres, the main building was two-storied with wood-shingled siding. Wrap-around verandas on both levels would afford a remarkable view of the ocean causeway and distant rain forest. A wooden boardwalk connected the main building to two smaller structures. A patio bar surrounded one end of the partially covered pool.

The sea air infused Jordan's exhausted body like a

shot of caffeine. "Do we have to wait for our luggage?"

Darcy turned back to her. "*Pas, mon petit*, they'll deliver it to our rooms."

"Guess I don't have to be concerned about that," Ellie grumbled. She marched ahead to the hotel entrance.

Seeing Darcy's raised eyebrow, Jordan explained, "The airline misplaced her luggage. She's a little cranky about it."

"I don't blame her. It's happened to me a time or three."

Entering the air-conditioned lobby, Jordan said, "Oh my God, this feels wonderful."

Ellie's pale skin erupted into goose bumps. She gave a slight shudder from the change in temperature. "Great. I don't even have a sweater."

Darcy eyed the lengthy registration line and suggested they browse the gift shop until it cleared. They crossed the Andalusa blue-and-white-patterned, tiled foyer and entered the shop.

A red tee shirt with *Roatán* and a glittering martini glass embroidered in silver sequins caught Ellie's eye. "I'm going to buy this. I can sleep in it tonight if my luggage doesn't arrive. See, Jordan, this is me trying to be cheerful." She forced a grin.

"I'm sure you'll look smashing in that outfit," Darcy assured her.

"Why, thank you, kind sir."

Jordan purchased bottled water for their room.

TARGETED   15

At the registration desk, Ellie asked the clerk to send her suitcase to their room as soon as the airline delivered it. The clerk made a note then handed out room key cards and resort activity sheets.

"We're on the second floor," Jordan confirmed, after looking at her card.

"Me, too," Darcy said. He punched the elevator up button. "It says on the activity sheet that Happy Hour is at six p.m. Will I see you both there?"

Ellie piped up with, "Wouldn't miss it!"

Burgundy-painted walls decorated with prints of ocean seascapes lined the second-floor hallway. The tiling in the lobby had been repeated on the hall flooring.

Darcy stopped halfway down the hall at his room. As the girls walked past him to their end unit and opened the door, he called out, "Remember to put the chain on your door."

Jordan waved a dismissive arm at him while waiting for Ellie to work the key card. She felt his eyes on her back as she followed Ellie inside and locked the door behind them.

CHAPTER 5

The water trickled from the shower head. Darcy banged on it, muttering, "Bloody hell." After drying off, he ran an electric shaver over his face then worked gel into his hair until the spiked row stood at attention. Satisfied with his mirror image, he donned Bermuda shorts and a tee shirt. The lousy water pressure had given him an excuse to see what the new hotel manager was up to.

On the main floor, he leaned against the wall outside the manager's office and craned his neck. A man in his early thirties paced back and forth, in and out of Darcy's line of vision. When the phone squawked, the manager dove across his desk to answer it. "Robson here."

Darcy plastered himself back against the wall and pretended to be engrossed in reading the resort's activity sheet.

"Chief Florés, have you made any progress in your investigation? No? I've had three calls from her family in London. They're worried sick."

There was silence for a minute before Darcy heard Robson drop into his chair. "Yes, I know you've conducted an extensive search of the island resorts and countryside, but that doesn't satisfy family members. Or me, for that matter. This is bad for business."

Darcy dared another look as Robson picked up a pen and stabbed his desk pad with it.

"I don't care if that seems like a cold remark to you. I don't have time for bull shit." A pause, then, "By all means, have your men tramp around the grounds again. Tell them to come to my office when they get here."

Robson's tone grew more forceful. "What do you mean her luggage was returned for me to courier to London? Where did your men put it? It had better turn up! *Adios*, Chief."

After a brief examination of Robson's door lock, Darcy sauntered back to the elevator, whistling the theme song from the 2013 movie, *Bounty Killer*. Now was not the time to mention plumbing problems.

CHAPTER 6

While Ellie dashed out to their balcony to drink in the view of the long dock below and the causeway out to sea, Jordan plunked her suitcase down on one of the beds and put away her clothes. Finished, she kicked off her sandals. Getting up at four a.m. for their flight had been a bitch. But it was worth it to reach the island with a good part of the afternoon still before them.

She was pleased with the décor of their air-conditioned suite. Gray-tiled floor and white-plastered walls gave the unit a clean, airy feeling. Bamboo blinds for the patio doors were mounted above the door frame.

She scoped out the bathroom and noticed that the window overlooked the pool bar area. On the far left, a silo-like metal structure sprouted like a rusty mushroom. Probably the water storage tank. Luckily, the ugly thing wasn't in direct view. She flopped onto her bed with a sigh of contentment.

A now-cheerful Ellie bounced into the room. "Do you need to use the bathroom before I jump in the shower?"

"No, thanks. I ducked into the lobby john while you were in the gift shop." Picking up the remote, she said, "I'll channel surf until you're done."

Hearing the squeaking twist of the faucet, Jordan raised her voice, "After our showers, let's put our bikinis on and hit the pool bar for a late lunch. I'm famished." She helped herself to a miniature, sweet banana from the bowl of fruit on their side table.

"Okay." A pause from Ellie, then, "Oh, come on!"

"What's the matter? Have a visit from a cute, little green lizard?"

"Nope. I think the shower head has prostate problems."

Jordan snickered. "Everyone who arrived with us is probably taking a shower. I'm sure the pressure will improve later."

A local newscast was starting. Jordan turned up the volume to hear over the faint water spray and the not-so-faint bars of "When You're Hot, You're Hot" emanating from the bathroom.

A Honduran journalist reported in English that four men had been arrested in connection with an island drug-

TARGETED   21

trafficking investigation. The sullen arrestees were filmed on La Ceiba Beach, being loaded into a beat-up police van. The camera zoomed in on the bicep of the last man to be shoved into the vehicle. He sported a dagger tattoo with red blood dripping onto the words *Madras 16*. Confirmation, the journalist said, that these men were linked to a local outlaw gang.

Next, he gravely announced that there were no new developments in the search for a British tourist, missing from Roatán for seven days. Jordan, bored with the depressing local news, was about to shut off the TV when she heard something that caused her to ramp up the volume. "Maryanne Reston, from London, England, had been staying at the Barefoot Bay resort when she disappeared."

When Ellie emerged with marigold yellow towels wrapped around her hair and body, Jordan turned off the TV and flung the remote down as if it had stung her. Since Ellie was in a snit over her lost luggage, now was not the time to tell her about the missing guest.

Ellie dropped her body towel and wiggled into her emerald-green bikini. She called over her shoulder, "It's your turn, buddy."

Jordan was relieved to see that Ellie had closed and latched the dark gray shutters over the bathroom window. Although, after watching the news broadcast, she would have preferred to see steel bars.

ഇരൗ

As they strolled along the boardwalk, they slid their sunglasses on to protect their eyes from the strong island sun. The poolside bar and grill drew them like an oasis in a desert. But no dashing Lawrence of Arabia waited to serve them. Instead, a squat bartender with a three-inch scar down the left side of his cheek said gruffly, "Afternoon, *señoritas*. What'll it be?"

Jordan asked, "Could we see lunch and drink menus, *por favor*?"

The man plopped plasticized menus in front of them and turned his back to dry beer glasses. A few minutes later, he leaned his solid, hairy arms on the bar and said, "I'm José. Have you made up your minds?"

"I'll have a mojito and tortillas *con quesillo*, José," Jordan said pleasantly.

"Make that two," Ellie added.

José shouted the food order into the window to the kitchen and busied himself mixing their cocktails. To avoid the leering glances he sent their way, the women swiveled their stools to face the pool. Ellie whispered to Jordan, "Freddy Keuger's got nothing on this guy."

Ellie jumped when José slammed their drinks on the bar behind them. "Two mojitos."

Reaching back for her drink, Jordan took a sip and felt the last of the tension seep from her weary body. Sun, beach, alcohol, and soon, food—life was good.

Ellie elbowed her in the ribs. "Whoa! Look at what's coming our way."

CHAPTER 7

A man strode in their direction with the assurance of a model walking a New York runway. His red polo shirt hugged wide shoulders and a slender waist. He greeted the guests lounging by the pool as he passed them.

Damn, if he didn't remind Jordan of Matthew McConaughey, dimples and all. He stopped in front of them, his high-wattage smile showing white, even teeth.

"Afternoon, ladies. I'm Tate Robson, hotel manager. Welcome to our island paradise."

"You're a lucky man to have such a fabulous work environment. I'm Jordan and this is Ellie."

He settled on the stool next to Ellie. "I see from your registration cards that you're fellow Ontarians."

"That's right," Ellie said as she gazed up into his hazel eyes. She licked the sugar from the rim of her cocktail glass.

Jordan jabbed her in the side with a sharp finger to remind her to behave.

"Well, you picked the perfect vacation spot, although I confess I'm slightly biased," Tate admitted. He nodded his thanks as José placed a tall glass of dark beer in his hand.

The bartender moved away and withdrew a cell phone from his shirt pocket. His brooding eyes remained glued on his boss and the two Canadian women as he conducted a hushed conversation in Spanish.

"I've been here two years and almost—notice I said almost—feel guilty accepting my pay checks."

"Where in Ontario are you from?" Ellie asked.

"I grew up in Parry Sound, graduated from the Hospitality and Tourism Management program at Algonquin College, then did my Masters at University of Western Ontario. Where do you both live?"

"Jordan lives at the Beaches in Toronto. I'm from Mississauga. We roomed together when we were undergrads at the University of Guelph."

Their conversation halted as José plunked their food down.

"I'll leave you to enjoy your meal. Let's talk later." Tate stood up, setting his empty glass on the bar. "I have an important phone call to make. Today is my mother's birthday, and she'd disown me if I didn't call her." He started to walk away then turned back. "Would you both join me for dinner this evening?"

"We'd love to, wouldn't we, Jordan?"

Jordan smiled and nodded. A thoughtful son with killer looks, intelligence, and a charming manner—what's not to like? She found herself looking forward to dinner, and she hadn't eaten lunch yet.

"Excellent. I'll meet you at 7:00 p.m. in the dining room. Just ask to be seated at my table."

"It's a date." The expression on Ellie's face would light up the darkest night.

As Tate opened the door to the lobby, she called out, "Mind if we bring another Canadian friend to dinner?"

"Not at all." He disappeared into the building.

Ellie hugged Jordan. "What a hunk. He made me forget to complain about our pathetic water pressure." She turned to signal for another cocktail.

"You can work that into our dinner conversation tonight if you run out of more interesting topics."

"Maybe after dinner, he'll come up and personally inspect our plumbing." Ellie teased as she sampled her second cocktail.

"Down, girl. He's probably married with a couple of *niños*."

"No way," Ellie said with finality. "My radar can detect a married man from a mile away. Besides, there's no wedding ring on his finger."

"You mean the radar that malfunctioned last summer with the guy you met at your cousin's wedding? You remember. The one with *tres niños*?"

Ellie threw a pretend punch at Jordan's shoulder. "That's not fair. All equipment malfunctions once in a while." She put her drink down and concentrated on shoveling the delectable Caribbean food into her mouth.

A movement overhead caught Jordan's attention. On the second floor, a leashed German shepherd dragged its uniformed handler along the veranda. Was it her imagination, or did the dog hesitate at their room before disappearing around the corner?

Jordan wondered if the dog was trained to sniff out drugs or bodies.

CHAPTER 8

Refreshed after a dip in the pool, they headed upstairs to change for the evening. Ellie entered the room first and tripped over an object left inside the door. She squealed with delight. "They found my suitcase. Thank God. Your clothes are way too big for me." Then she tried to withdraw her foot from her mouth. "Not that I don't appreciate the offer. Be right back. Got to pee."

Jordan laid the suitcase on Ellie's bed and flipped over the tag. Her heart plummeted. Maryanne Reston. She dropped the tag.

"Ellie, I hate to be the bearer of bad news, but this isn't your suitcase."

The bathroom door flew open and Ellie stormed out.

"What? Are you sure, Jordan? It looks like mine."

Jordan explained that the suitcase belonged to a resort guest the authorities have been searching for since last week. "I heard about this when I was watching the news earlier. The room number on the tag is correct, so she—Maryanne Reston—must have stayed in our room."

"Well, now, that's just creepy!" Ellie groaned as she sunk down on her bed.

"I'll take this luggage down to the desk clerk. Yours has probably been delivered to someone else's room."

"Guess I'll need to borrow your white mini-skirt tonight after all," she said sheepishly.

"Not so picky now, are we? Why don't you change, then ring Darcy's room and invite him to join us for dinner while I run this suitcase downstairs?"

"We're already meeting him for drinks at Happy Hour, but okay." Never disheartened for long, Ellie hurried over to place the call.

⁂

Dragging the suitcase along like a stubborn puppy, Jordan bypassed the registration desk and tapped lightly on Tate's open door.

"Come in." He pushed an errant lock of chestnut hair off his forehead and grinned when he saw who his visitor was. "Jordan, have a seat. What can I do for you?"

He swept up the sheets of paper fanned out on his

desk and dropped them into his center desk drawer. Before the drawer slammed shut, she noticed two passports among the heap.

She perched on the edge of the chair and released her grip on the suitcase.

"We found this luggage inside our room. The airline misplaced Ellie's. We thought it was hers until I checked the tag."

Tate reached for his phone. "I'll have it sent to the proper room."

"Before you make that call, there's something else you should know."

He lowered the phone slowly to its cradle.

Jordan inhaled a deep breath before continuing. "The luggage belongs to your missing guest, Maryanne Reston. I heard about her disappearance on the local newscast."

Tate twirled his chair to reach the liquor decanter on his side cabinet. He poured two fingers into a glass and gulped it down before turning back to face Jordan. Noticing her surprised expression, he blurted out, "I'm—I'm sorry. Can I offer you some brandy? Not waiting for her response, he added, "Or I can get you a ginger ale from the vending machine."

"Nothing, thanks, I'm fine."

"The police were to deliver that suitcase to me after they concluded their examination. I'll have it shipped to her family if she doesn't return for it soon."

"So you think there's a chance she'll show up?"

"Stranger things have happened. She may have had a romantic interlude with one of the yacht skippers parked at our dock and gone sailing for the week."

Little beads of sweat popped out on his tanned forehead. He seemed to be taking this woman's disappearance very personally.

"It's a bit unnerving being in this missing woman's room."

"I understand. Would you like to change rooms?"

"I appreciate the offer, but we're settled in now." As she rose to leave, she noticed a bronze statue of a parrot beside his liquor decanter. She leaned down to read the inscription, *To Tate Robson, for Managerial Excellence.* "You must be very proud of this commendation." She reached out to touch the sculpture's beak. Before her fingers made contact, Tate shot up and steered her out of his office. "I'm sure every hotel manager in the Caribbean has one of these."

"You're far too modest," she countered as he propelled her to the elevator.

"I'm sorry about the suitcase mix-up and your room allocation. What can I do to make it up to you?"

Before Jordan could respond, a man wearing an orange shirt with *Maintenance* stitched on the pocket, walked up behind them.

"Actually, there is something you could do for me. We have very little water pressure in our shower."

CHAPTER 9

"Wa—water pressure?" Tate stumbled over the words.

The workman addressed his boss. "I'll see to that immediately, Señor Robson."

"Thanks, Carlos. You saved me having to page you."

"That would be wonderful, thank you. It's Room twenty-five," Jordan said.

Carlos nodded and sauntered down the hallway. Tate withdrew his hand from Jordan's elbow as the elevator door opened.

"I'll call the airline and see if I can track down Ellie's luggage."

"Thanks, Tate. See you at dinner." As the elevator rose, Jordan replayed their conversation in her mind and

Tate's air of tension. By the time she reached her room, she chalked up his odd behavior to concern over bad publicity for the hotel.

❧❧❧

Their suite looked like a tornado had swept through and deposited an entire landfill. Stepping over clothes to peer into the bathroom, Jordan saw that Ellie had indeed borrowed her white skirt and favorite black sequined top. But not before trying on and discarding everything else Jordan owned.

"Geez, Ellie. Have problems making up your mind about what to borrow?"

"Sorry about that. I didn't want to keep you waiting." Ellie sent Jordan an apologetic grin before turning back to the mirror to sweep brown mascara onto her lashes.

Jordan changed into a navy silk mini-skirt and a matching top with spaghetti-straps. She re-folded her abused clothes and put them away. Using the wall mirror, she twisted her hair into a neat chignon, fastening it with a blue sequined butterfly clip. Finally, she dusted her nose and cheekbones with bronzing powder and applied a raspberry lip gloss.

There, done. In this humidity, the less makeup, the better.

Ellie sang out, "I'm almost ready. I just have to let my hair down."

"I hope you mean that literally," Jordan said, only half joking.

"You haven't seen anything yet, my uptight friend. Wait until tonight after Happy Hour." Ellie unbraided and ran a brush through her wavy tresses before inserting large, gold hoop earrings into her ear lobes. She danced out the door, crooking her finger in a "follow me" motion at Jordan.

Jordan vowed to herself that their first evening in paradise was *not* going to end badly. She regretted the absence of her handcuffs.

CHAPTER 10

Jordan's laughter bubbled out at something Ellie whispered to her. Darcy envied their carefree mood and wished that his trip here didn't have a dark side. With two fingers to his lips, he blew a piercing whistle to get their attention. When they looked up, he waved them over to his table on the patio. "You two look delicious enough to eat."

"Why, thank you, Mr. Wolf," Ellie responded, tossing him her come-hither look. "You look hot yourself."

He had changed into beige chino pants and a violet, short-sleeved dress shirt.

Darcy signalled to José and ordered three Coronas. When the drinks arrived, they downed the cold brews with relish. As the steel band struck up the Merrymen's "Feeling Hot, Hot, Hot" chords, conversation was put on the back burner.

Ellie yanked him from the comfort of his chair. "Why, Darcy, I do believe they're playing our song."

He glanced back at Jordan and held out his hand for her to join them.

"You two go ahead. I'm fine sitting here, people watching."

After the dance set ended, Darcy led a flushed Ellie to the bar for refills before returning to their table. He sat down, unfastening another two buttons on his shirt to cool off.

"Darcy, did you catch today's news about a woman who has been missing for a week from this resort?" Jordan asked.

Darcy took a swig of beer before answering. "I did see that. Unsettling news for sure."

"Doesn't exactly make me feel warm and fuzzy about safety around here," Ellie sighed before motioning to José again.

"Better pace yourself, Ellie. The night is young," Jordan cautioned.

"Yes, and so are we. Remember?"

When José trudged to their table, Jordan said, "I'll have an iced tea this time."

"Make that two," Darcy added.

"Another one of these," Ellie held up her empty bottle.

José grunted and re-traced his steps to the bar.

Searching for a more upbeat topic, Darcy said, "Speaking of age. I'll bet you two still get carded at bars."

"Can't say that hasn't happened a few times," Ellie said. "How old are you, Darcy?"

"I'm thirty. Old enough to know better, but young enough not to care what people think."

"We're both twenty-eight, but Jordan is six months older." Seeing Jordan's frown, she quickly added, "Jordan doesn't like me to discuss her private business, so, changing the subject, do you have poor water pressure in your shower? Ours sucks."

"Ditto. There was barely water enough to refresh my pits."

He leaned back in his chair and locked his fingers behind his head. His right bicep swelled and a dragon's tail writhed. Ellie convulsed into giggles. He noticed Jordan's eyes roll before she feigned interest in watching José deliver their beverages.

Darcy squeezed a lemon slice into his iced tea. "I'll report the pressure problem tomorrow."

"No need," Jordan assured him. "A guy from maintenance overheard me when I complained to Tate. He's taking care of it."

He didn't miss her use of the manager's first name. "Splendid. I'm looking forward to meeting this Tate guy over dinner. There was a different bloke in charge when I was here three years ago." He consulted his watch. "It's almost seven. Let's hit the food trough while the band is on break."

Ellie said, "I'm starving and I'm sure Jordan is eager to see Tate again." She stood up to follow Darcy then grabbed the table with her hand to steady herself. "I must have had too much sun," she snorted, then caught up to him and gripped the back of his shoulders.

He stopped dead, not sure what she had in mind.

"Piggyback me to my seat." She jumped on his back and wrapped her arms and legs around him.

"Hold on tight then." He whinnied and galloped over to the dining room entrance.

Jordan caught up with them as he was encouraging Ellie to dismount. She addressed the maître d'. "Mr. Robson asked that we be seated at his table."

They were led to a white wicker table by the window. The glass top was set for four.

Jordan sank into her chair and picked up the wine menu to avoid making eye contact with Ellie. Darcy heard her mutter under her breath, "Oh, man. This is going to be a long night."

CHAPTER 11

A mix of tantalizing aromas wafted from the buffet table, causing Jordan's stomach to grumble in anticipation. Too many hours had passed and too much liquor had hit her gut since their highly seasoned lunch.

"That bird resembles the award in Tate's office." She gestured at a parrot perched on a stand. Its plumage was brilliant. Red feathers covered the back of its head, feathers on his neck were green bleeding into blue on its back, and the long tail feathers were a combination of black and red. It danced from foot to foot, as if its perch was hot, while eyeing guests circling the buffet tables.

"That's a Scarlet Macaw. Honduras' national bird," Darcy said. "What was Tate's award for? Charming the pants off the most female guests in the Caribbean?" He winked at Ellie.

Ellie choked on her sip of water.

Jordan gave Darcy a hard look. "It's an award for his management expertise."

"I think you misread it," Darcy countered. His smile didn't quite reach his Arctic-blue eyes. Noticing her looking over his shoulder, he turned to see what had bagged her attention.

Tate paused at the entrance to the dining room, surveying the crowd like a king holding court. There was a sudden cessation in conversation by most of the females.

Ellie whispered to Jordan, "Now, there is some serious eye candy."

Tate's black slacks hugged his form in all the right places. His short-sleeved, silk black shirt was open to the swell of his muscular chest. When he reached their table, he smiled, and a dimple appeared in one cheek. Jordan's pulse quickened when he sent her a sexy smile.

Darcy cleared his throat to pry Robson's eyes away from Jordan before standing up. "I'm Darcy Piermont. You must be Tate Robson."

The men shook hands, and Jordan noticed they both squeezed a little, the way men do when their testosterone is spiking. Two alpha males posturing for female attention. She saw plenty of pissing contests in her line of work. It might be an interesting night after all.

Tate was an inch or two taller, but Darcy had a more

TARGETED 41

athletic build. It was anyone's guess which guy would win in a throw-down fight.

Ellie was practically drooling. Jordan fingered her glass of water and contemplated tossing it over her friend to cool her down. On second thought, she better save some for herself.

"Glad you could join us. What part of Canada are you from?"

Darcy released the other man's hand and sat down. "Born and raised in Montreal."

"A lovely city for sure. I have a college friend who lives there, so I've visited a couple of times." Tate gently removed the wine menu from Jordan's grasp and set it down. "Allow me to order wine from my private stock. White or red?"

"I'm in the mood for a red wine," Ellie said.

"Fine by me," Jordan concurred.

"Cool," Darcy added, although Robson hadn't addressed him.

Tate motioned to a hovering waiter. "Ramon, two bottles of *Calvario*, *por favor*."

"*Si,* Señor Robson."

The dining room was alive with chatter. Guests who had partaken of the rum punch at Happy Hour were still in party mode.

"What was your mother doing to celebrate her birthday?" asked Ellie while she watched for Ramon to return with the wine.

"Her book club members surprised her by coming over with chili, cake, and from the inflection of her voice, I'd say a shitload of wine."

"How thoughtful, but still, I bet she missed you not being there," Ellie said.

"I've bought her a plane ticket to come here and visit me for two weeks at the end of the month. That should make up for my not being with her today."

Ramon returned, cradling the wine in one hand like a newborn baby and carrying an ice bucket in the other. He uncorked the wine and presented it to Tate. Tate inclined his head at Darcy, and Ramon hurried over to pour an inch of ruby liquid into his glass.

Darcy waved the wine's bouquet toward his nose with his hand then placed his nose to the rim of the glass and sniffed noisily. He took a mouthful and gargled before swallowing. Jordan stifled a snicker. What an ass!

The Montreal native looked at Tate and nodded his approval. "A nice Spanish wine with a fragrance of toasty oak, and a mild flavor of wild blackberry with floral undertones."

Ramon filled their glasses then backed away to tend to other guests.

"*Salud.* To an evening of stimulating conversation and fine dining with fellow Canadians," Tate toasted.

Jordan loved the clink of fine crystal. It made her tingle with celebratory anticipation. After a few sips, even Darcy began to look good to her.

TARGETED 43

She shook her head. She definitely needed to get some food into her stomach pronto.

Tate said, "You have a knowledgeable palate for quality wines, Darcy."

"I've sampled many good wines while in Madrid overseeing my Hooters bar."

Tate's eyes widened. Jordan was beginning to think she had fallen down a rabbit hole, and Darcy was the Mad Hatter. She reached for her wine glass again and took a deeper swallow. Darcy acted as though he was living a Bond movie. Hmmm, Matthew McConaughey and a blond, spikey-haired James Bond as dinner dates. She could do worse. And, were they going to eat some time tonight?

Ellie patted Darcy's thigh approvingly. "So you own a tattoo parlor in Montreal and a Hooters bar in Madrid. You're a man of many talents, aren't you?"

"I get bored easily. My third business isn't nearly as interesting."

Ellie opened her mouth, no doubt to ask Darcy to elaborate.

Jordan kicked her ankle under the table. There was no need for Ellie to encourage him.

"Ow!" Ellie shot Jordan a reproachful look. Jordan lobbed back a *Change-the-subject-for-God's-sake* glare.

Darcy noticed the friction between them and got up. "Let's put on the old feed bag."

"I'm with you," Ellie said with Mary Poppins-like enthusiasm. She sprang from her chair and linked her arm through Darcy's to steady herself.

Jordan managed to make it to the head of the line by elbowing Darcy and Ellie out of the way. She expected Tate would be right behind her, but he remained seated and poured another expensive glass of wine. He passed them on their way back to their table as they balanced a tower of food on their plates.

CHAPTER 12

After his guests sampled their food assortment, Tate asked their opinion on the buffet selection. Barely swallowing his mouthful, Darcy mumbled, "*Bon merci*, but I'm disappointed there is no poutine."

Ellie laughed and lightly ran a finger up the dolphin tattoo on his left bicep.

"Poutine is a coronary on a plate," Tate admonished. "Island fare is much healthier."

"I can't disagree with you there, old chap, but it's a diet staple in Quebec."

Jordan visualized Tate and Darcy as two polite duelists facing off in an historical movie. One of them generally ended up shot to death or stabbed with a sword.

Even Ellie realized a change of topic was in order. "Let's play Truth or Dare while we eat," she suggested. "It's a good way to get to know each other."

"You scare me with the dare part. I vote we stick to the truth," Jordan pleaded.

"Oh, all right. We'll play by your rules this time," Ellie sighed theatrically. "I'll start." She threw an impish look at both men. "I'm single and available."

Darcy said, "Truth."

Ellie slapped the table with the flat of her hand. "You're too good at this, Darcy. It's your turn."

"I'm married with three kids."

"False," the diners chimed in unison.

"Well, you got me there, but it's partially true. I was married for about five minutes many years ago."

"What happened to your wife?" Jordan asked before she could stop herself.

"*Cherie*, take my word for it. Don't be romanced into a quickie wedding in Vegas. Even if the Elvis Chapel is having a discount sale." Darcy enjoyed the surprised reaction on his companions' faces. "You're up, Jordan."

She thought for a minute. "Okay. My favorite course in university was Topography."

Ellie whooped then clapped a hand over her mouth. Between her fingers, she said, "Sorry, I'll have to pass on this one."

Tate said, "True."

"False," Darcy tapped his water glass with his fork for emphasis.

"Darcy's right. It was Criminology," Jordan admitted.

"Tate, it's your turn," Ellie said, twisting a long, red strand of hair around her finger.

"Oh, well, let me see. Okay—my favorite hobby is chess."

"Correct," Darcy wagered.

"Nope. It's Caribbean Poker."

"Let's stop now before we get to know each other too well," Jordan said.

"If you insist." Ellie pretended to pout then broke into an infectious giggle.

Darcy leaned forward to peer into Jordan's golden brown eyes. "What do you and Ellie do when you're not vacationing on an island paradise?"

Ellie butted in. "I'm marketing manager for my family's business in Toronto. We're importers of teas and spices."

Jordan was reticent to talk about her line of work to strangers but, since three pair of eyes studied her, finally said quietly, "I'm with the Toronto Police Service."

"In the Guns and Gang Task Force," Ellie added proudly.

A stillness fell over the table. Followed by a choking, gagging sound.

CHAPTER 13

Darcy tried to swallow, but his esophagus clamped around the chunk of spicy prawn and held it fast. He fought down panic and tried to take a breath through his clogged windpipe. No air in—no prawn out! He jumped up, knocking his chair over, and clutched his throat. As his vision dimmed, he heard a calm, female voice command, "Step back, I've got this."

Arms wrapped around his abdomen from the back. Fingers felt for the spot above his navel. Two fists pushed in and upward. Darcy felt a violent squeezing sensation. The offending prawn shot out of his gullet, flew across the table, and knocked Tate's wine glass over. Then instant relief. Tate looked down at the partially chewed shrimp with disgust and covered it with his napkin.

Air entered Darcy's lungs and oxygen flowed back to his brain. He slowly lowered himself back into the chair that Ellie had righted for him. He picked up his napkin to mop the tears streaming down his face. In a hoarse voice, he whispered, "Well, that was quite the ice breaker, wasn't it?" Noting the concerned faces of his dinner companions and other guests sitting nearby, he threw both hands over his head, fingers spread in the "V" for victory sign. The room erupted in applause and cheering.

When the noise died down, he looked across the table at Jordan, giving her a feeble grin. "Thanks for coming to my rescue." His voice sounded like Kermit the Frog's.

"My pleasure," Jordan replied.

He noticed her hands had a slight tremor as she reached for her water glass.

Tate discreetly pushed the napkin-covered prawn under a bread plate. "Are you sure you're all right, Piermont? Perhaps the resort doctor should have a look at you."

"I'm fine now, Robson. But thanks." Darcy cleared his raw throat and took another sip of water. "So, Jordan, you're a cop."

"That I am," she replied.

"A noble profession for sure," Tate said then changed the subject. "Anyone for dessert and coffee?"

Darcy noticed that Robson had barely touched his first course. "I'm going to cruise for something cold to soothe my throat."

Ellie and Jordan followed Darcy to the dessert tables.

TARGETED   51

The women selected fried bananas in brown sugar sauce with golden pineapple wedges on the side. Tate passed on dessert, opting for another glass of *Calvario*.

Feeling more like himself again, Darcy pushed his empty mango sherbet dish away and stifled a burp of satisfaction. "Pardon me. Anyone up for a ramble down the dock to the gazebo? You know, to burn off some of the calories we've ingested? And, in my case, to recover from a near death experience."

"Count me in," Ellie agreed with fervor.

Tate stood up. "It's been delightful dining with you but, please, excuse me. I have some business to attend to. Would you like to accompany me tomorrow evening to a casino in La Ceiba?"

"We'll pass, Tate, but thanks for the invite. There isn't any wiggle room in our budget for gambling," Jordan replied. She looked pointedly at Ellie.

"No problem, we can get together another evening for drinks." Tate motioned for the waiter to bring the bar bill for him to sign. "Enjoy the rest of your evening," he said as he pushed his chair back and left the dining room.

Jordan put her hand over her mouth to mask a yawn. "Count me out of the stroll, Darcy. I'm beat."

Ellie re-applied a coat of lip gloss and fluffed her shock of hair. "It looks like it's you and me, Darcy."

"It appears so. Sweet dreams, Jordan." He helped Ellie up from her chair and watched Jordan make for the exit.

Ellie called, "Don't wait up for me, Mom."

"Have fun, kids," Jordan called back.

"Let's stop at the bar on our way out," Ellie implored.

"As you wish, *chérie*."

She ordered a Spanish coffee to go. Darcy requested an apple juice. He needed to keep his wits about him to avoid getting into a compromising situation with Ellie. She was tanked and dangerously playful. And he had no time for games tonight.

CHAPTER 14

Outside, Jordan paused to let the humid evening breeze off the ocean caress her skin. She gazed longingly at the gently rolling waves visiting the sandy beach. If she wasn't dead on her feet and slightly inebriated, she would remove her sandals and wade along the water's edge. Sadly, her need for sleep won out.

Hours later, she pushed herself up onto an elbow and attacked the pillow with her fist. She was exhausted so why couldn't she get back to sleep? She rolled over and looked at the bedside clock radio. It was 1:00 a.m. and Ellie's bed was empty. A female guest was missing, and a cop from a canine unit had been searching the premises. Would Ellie be safe with Darcy?

She chided herself for being a mother hen and coaxed

her weary eyes to close. Minutes later, they fluttered open at a muffled sound from the hallway. She padded over and opened the door wide enough to stick her head out. Maybe Ellie was returning from Darcy's room and needed help getting into bed. But no Ellie. Instead, she saw Darcy's back as he jogged to the elevator.

Perhaps Ellie had fallen asleep in his room, and he was going to the ice machine. But why did he have a travel bag slung over his shoulder?

Jordan hurriedly exchanged PJs for shorts and tee shirt. After stuffing her key card in a pocket, she crept down the hall and entered the stairwell.

On the lobby level, she cracked the door and spied Darcy standing by the vending machine outside the closed gift shop. He pretended to look for change in his pocket until a young couple, arms wrapped lovingly around each other's waist, walked by. Crossing the lobby to Tate's office, he extracted a flathead screwdriver from his bag and inserted it into the door lock. Leaning down, he put his right ear close to the lock as he twisted the tool, waited a few seconds, and withdrew it. Next, he reached into the side zippered pocket of his tote. He withdrew a paperclip, straightened it, then bent one end. He inserted the improvised pick into the lock and worked it.

A moment later, he pulled the paperclip out and turned the knob. The door opened. Straightening up, he glanced behind him once more before entering. The door closed softly behind him.

TARGETED

Jordan was struck by indecision—an unaccustomed sensation. Should she confront him? Should she find Tate? Should she ignore her cop instincts and mind her own business?

Option one would be foolhardy. She wasn't armed, not even with a baton. Option two seemed plausible, but a gut feeling made her hesitate.

Option three won out. For now. She ran up the stairs to her room. As she opened the door, an unexpected sound made her jump.

Ellie was in her bed, snoring her drunken little head off.

CHAPTER 15

Jordan watched a catamaran, filled with excited passengers, glide out the causeway into the aqua waters of West Bay.

She longed to be with them instead of standing on the veranda waiting for Ellie to surface from her alcohol-induced stupor.

A tortured groan behind her broke her reverie. Ellie attempted to roll over. It wasn't pretty. She opened one green eye, now shot through with red, then shut it again. She struggled a second time to sit up.

"Holy shit, Jordan. Close that freaking blind! I have the mother of all hangovers."

Jordan took her time lowering the blinds. "The morning is half over. Rise and shine."

Ellie gingerly placed her head back down on her pillow, face first. "Oh, man."

"I'll take that as a no. I'm going downstairs for breakfast. I'll check back on you in an hour."

Ellie grunted then began a new bout of snoring. Her wild mass of hair splayed across the pillow. She looked like she had been caught in an electrical storm. Leaning over Ellie's bed, Jordan turned the unconscious face to the side so her friend wouldn't smother.

As she placed her hand on the door knob, a loud rap from the other side startled her. She opened the door to the extent of the safety chain. A smiling Honduran porter stood outside with a black suitcase in hand.

Jordan slipped the chain and stepped into the hall just as Ellie came to life again and called out, "If that isn't a hot guy with a Bloody Mary, I'll strangle the bastard."

She crash-landed back onto her pillow. Jordan hastily closed the door before another string of profanity vaulted from Sleeping Beauty's lips.

"*Señor* Tate said to bring this right up to you, *señorita*."

"*Gracias.*"

Jordan pulled the suitcase inside and leaned it against Ellie's bed. She held her breath as she checked the name tag. Thank God, this time it was the right one. Now her clothes were her own again.

ოჳოჳ

It felt deliciously sinful to be eating breakfast out-doors in shorts and a halter top. Back home on her day off, Jordan would be wearing jeans and a warm jacket. On the job, she sweated under a Kevlar vest, with sixteen pounds of equipment hanging from her belt.

Her meal of half a pink grapefruit, a slice of brown toast, scrambled eggs, and rich Honduran coffee added to her contentment. She ordered a second cup of coffee and reached for her eReader. She read several pages of *Corpse Flower,* a laugh-out-loud mystery by a Canadian author, before the harsh scrape of metal across patio stones broke her concentration.

Darcy swung his leg over the back of a chair and plunked down beside her. "Morning, sunshine," he said amiably. "What's with the frown lines on that lovely brow of yours?"

"I was engrossed in my novel," Jordan retorted. Should she mention last night?

"Didn't mean to startle you. How are you feeling this beautiful morning?" He waved the waitress over.

"I couldn't be better, thanks. I can't say the same for Ellie, though." She waited while he ordered a brunch that would feed a family of four.

"Poor little bird. I'm sorry to hear she's under the weather."

His pineapple yellow tee shirt proclaimed in black let-ters: *Nobody Makes Me Drink. I'm a Volunteer.* He didn't seem to be the worse for wear after tying one on last night, before breaking into Tate's office.

"Since you partied together, I'm surprised you're not in the same condition."

"Whoa. Not guilty as charged. After a twenty-minute walk to the end of the dock and back, I returned our little party girl to the pool bar. Then went to my room. Alone."

"My apologies. I saw you walking down the hall in the wee hours of this morning and Ellie wasn't back so I assumed she was in your room."

He ignored her mention of his nighttime trek. "I did see your Tate leaning against the bar when I left Ellie last night."

"I guess a manager doesn't keep office hours. And he's not *my* Tate."

"If you say so. I should probably mind my own business, but you take a lot upon those lovely shoulders of yours, trying to keep Ellie out of mischief."

"Ellie and I look out for each other," she snapped then added, "And you're right. It's not your concern."

His smile dialed down a few notches. "Commendable, but not practical. Just saying."

Darcy's food arrived and Jordan took that as her cue to leave. When she stood up, Darcy reached out and touched her arm. "You know, Jordan, in some cultures, if you save a man's life, you own him forever."

Jordan snorted and shook off his hand. "In that case, I hereby set you free. I have a cat and don't need another pet around the house, especially a French poodle trained with English commands."

"*Touché* and pip, pip." He blinked a couple of times at the unexpected dig. "I must say that you're beginning to intrigue me. Your intellect, along with your wit and beauty, make an alluring package."

"Well, this package is labeled, 'Hands Off'!" With that, she marched to the lobby door.

Unrepentant, Darcy called after her, "I've a meeting at one p.m. but I'll save us a table at Happy Hour."

Over her shoulder, she raised her middle finger.

Who has meetings while on vacation anyway? And, why did he break into Tate's office? You didn't have to be a cop to realize something shady was going on. And she could do without the mind games he was trying to trick her into playing. It would take more than the flattery from a full-of-himself playboy to get her to drop her guard.

CHAPTER 16

Still fuming from Darcy's unsolicited advice and sorry attempt at flirtation, Jordan tiptoed past a comatose Ellie. She settled into a chair on the veranda to resume her reading.

A heated conversation drifted up from the dock beyond the bar and pool area. Once again, she set her eReader down.

Tate and two uniformed officers stood beside a police boat. Judging from the hand gestures, grim expressions, and raised voices, the men weren't happy campers. Tate shook his head before wheeling away and stomping toward the hotel. The cops climbed into their boat and drove off. Had they brought news about Maryanne Reston's disappearance?

Feeling slightly more charitable toward Ellie, Jordan made a trip to the gift shop to purchase antacids for her. On her way back, she hesitated by the elevator as a seasoned-looking police officer sidestepped around a parked laundry cart and knocked on Darcy's door. His crested head poked out and Darcy ushered the man in before closing the door. Then the door opened again and Darcy dragged the laundry cart inside.

Jordan approached his door, putting her ear against it, and listened. Only a muffled discourse could be heard. She went on to her own unit, having decided on a course of action regarding Ellie sleeping away their first day on the island.

გ∂ℰ∂

Jordan sprinkled cold water on Ellie's face then jumped back. Ellie jolted upright, fists swinging, before toppling off the bed. She crawled aimlessly in circles before using the bedpost to haul herself to her feet. She stubbed her baby toe on the bed frame.

"Ouch, shit!"

Jordan reached for the TV remote after Ellie staggered to the bathroom. She set it back down, picking up a brochure instead. Who needed more news about the local criminal element? This was her week away from having to deal with slime buckets.

Ellie came out carrying a bottle of water in one hand

and Tylenol in the other. She flashed a half-hearted smile at Jordan before swallowing two pain killers.

"Oh, man, I'm not sure I'm going to live."

Jordan handed her the package of antacids. "Take one of these and drink lots to dilute the alcohol in your system. So who was your date last night?"

"When Darcy pooped out on me, I ran into Tate in the bar. He invited me to go with him to a casino."

"That must have been fun for you since you don't gamble."

"Not a problem. I entertained myself. Met a cute sailor at the bar, and we played a drinking game or two. I finally dragged Tate away from the card tables around midnight. A friend of his drove us back to the island in his speed boat."

"So Tate put you to bed?"

"Must have since the last thing I remember was the very fast boat ride, and I'm still in the clothes I borrowed from you. Ah, sorry for the wrinkles" She looked down at the bodice of her top. "And the stains."

"Don't sweat it. Tonight, you've got your own clothes to wear." Setting the brochure down, Jordan sighed, "I'd love to go snorkeling today. But with your queasy stomach, guess it'll have to be another time."

"You think?" Ellie chortled, as she tossed a second antacid tablet into her mouth.

"Suit up and we'll go down to the pool bar and get you some tomato juice and dry toast to settle your stomach. Then we'll spend a glorious day on the beach doing frigging nothing."

Jordan changed into her red bikini and waited on the veranda while Ellie showered.

"Yeehaw!" Ellie shouted. "The water pressure is fantastic now. Just what did you do for Tate to get this fixed?"

Stepping out to their balcony, Jordan said, "I simply brought the problem to the attention of one of his maintenance staff."

From the corner of her eye, she noticed an ambulance drive slowly from the back of the resort to the road. *Sans* lights or siren—not a good sign. She hoped another guest's holiday hadn't ended badly.

CHAPTER 17

How does your head feel now, Ellie?"

"The hair from the dog that bit me last night has done the trick."

Jordan flipped her sunglasses down and snuggled into her lounge chair. "Good to hear."

Ellie dropped her empty Bloody Mary glass onto the sand. "What's Spanish for keep the drinks coming? Our cabaña boy seems to have forgotten us."

"Perhaps you should order a virgin drink so your liver can recover from last night."

"I'll be fine as long as I don't start tossing shooters again."

The male waiter serving guests by the pool made a 180 degree turn and headed their way. "Afternoon *señori-*

tas, can I interest you in our specialty drink of the day?"

Ellie grabbed two frosted Yellow Bird cocktails from the proffered tray then seemingly remembered her manners. "*Gracias*, your timing couldn't be better."

She aimed a dazzling smile at the cheerful waiter, who thrust a handful of napkins at them before moving to the next group of sun worshippers.

∞∞∞

Jordan's vision of sunning on an ocean beach, reading, and sipping tropical cocktails was finally a reality. She felt the weariness from yesterday's travel melt as quickly as the ice in her drink.

A shadow fell across her legs, and she looked up. A pleasant-looking teenager stood at the foot of her lounge chair grinning down at her. She took note of his nervous demeanor and clean island attire of cut-off blue jeans and a fern-patterned, short-sleeved shirt.

Since he didn't have a string of beaded necklaces dangling from his arm, she was curious to see just what he was peddling.

She smiled up at him while he worked up the nerve to make his pitch.

"*Hola*, beautiful American ladies. My name is Manuel Playla. I would love to be your tour guide this afternoon."

"You're half right, amigo," Ellie responded. "We're Canadian."

TARGETED 69

"Oh, damn. So sorry. I am Ladino or Mestizo," a flustered Manuel responded.

"That's a mix of American Indian and Spanish descents, isn't it?" Jordan asked.

"*Sí*," the young man confirmed. "I've always wanted to go to Canada. Maybe someday I'll get there. My wheels are parked in front of the hotel. Let me escort you on a private tour of our incredible island."

Encouraged by Ellie's brazen stare, he forged on. "I have *cervezas* on ice. My tour rates are the best on the island."

"And, just what would you charge to show us a good time?" Ellie asked, her voice smoldering with promise.

Once again, Jordan was tempted to pour the rest of her iced drink over Ellie.

"My special rate for you lovely *señoritas* is thirty dollars US each for a two-hour tour into our beautiful Sierra Madres mountain range. The view from 9,000 feet will take your breath away."

Bending to extract a cover-up from her bag, Ellie shot a glance over to gauge Jordan's reaction. "I can think of better ways to become breathless, but a *cerveza* or ten sounds perfect in this heat. As long as we're back in time for Happy Hour."

"*Sí*, No problem," Manuel assured them.

Jordan wasn't sure it would be smart to leave the resort with a local, no matter how innocent-looking. On the other hand, she wasn't certain staying at the hotel was all that safe either. Her friend's enthusiasm, and her own desire to see more of the island, swayed her decision. She nodded, setting her glass down before pulling her cover-up on and grabbing her tote.

Manuel beamed as Ellie thrust $60 cash into his hand. "You're on, my friend. By the way, I'm Ellie and this is Jordan."

Manuel helped Ellie stand as Jordan said, "We have to make a stop at the lobby first. We'll meet you out front in fifteen minutes."

A slight frown visited the young man's face as he called out, "I'll be waiting for you at my Jeep."

CHAPTER 18

In the lobby, they made a rest room stop. On the way out, Ellie said, "I want to speak to Tate."

Before Jordan could comment, Ellie hurried over and knocked softly on his doorframe before walking in.

"Well, what a lovely surprise. Come sit down."

Ellie winked before flashing him a generous smile. "Sorry, we can't stay. We're heading out on a tour of the island, but we'll catch up with you at Happy Hour."

"Did you book your tour through the front desk?"

"No, a charming Honduran teen approached us on the beach and offered a two-hour tour at a reasonable rate," Jordan explained.

"Not a good idea," Tate cautioned. "Locals have been known to rob tourists and leave them stranded in the mountains. Crime rates are somewhat lower on this island than the mainland. But violence and robbery are still a way of life here."

"We'll be fine. Our tour guide looks like he's barely reached puberty," Ellie assured him as they turned to leave.

Tate said, "Hold on a second." He opened a drawer in his side cabinet and withdrew a paper bag. "Here, at least take this with you."

"Thanks," Jordan said. She dropped the closed bag into her tote. Always good to have extra bottled water.

A rag-top Jeep, no stranger to fender-benders, idled at the curb. Manuel leaned against the vehicle, smoking. When he saw the women leave the resort's foyer, he tossed his butt to the asphalt and opened the passenger side door. He helped Ellie climb into the back seat before ushering Jordan into shotgun position. He leaned over and opened the lid of a cooler behind the driver's seat. By tossing a cold beer to Ellie, he became her new best friend. Jordan accepted a can of iced tea.

Climbing in without opening the door, Manuel put the Jeep into drive and gunned it. Jordan glanced at the side mirror and saw Tate standing outside the hotel entrance. He looked at his watch and then wrote something in a notepad.

CHAPTER 19

This is Coxen Hole," Manuel shouted over the drone of the motor as they sped through the village. Chickens scattered to the sides of the road as the Jeep made a sharp turn up the mountain road that would take them into the rain forest.

Jordan inhaled the intoxicating aroma of tropical foliage mixed with salty, ocean air. When Manuel slowed for a holy-shit turn, she caught a glimpse of a Toucan in a mangrove tree and, minutes later, a prehistoric-looking Iguana crawled onto a rock on the side of the road. Fascinated by the foreign jungle sights, smells, and songs of exotic birds, Jordan raised her voice over the hum of the motor. "What are the island's industries other than tourism?"

"Mainly bananas and coffee. We also export seafood, palm oil, fruit, and some corn and rice."

Ellie leaned forward and patted Manuel's right shoulder. "You're not only easy on the eyes, you're smart, too. And did I forget to mention hot?"

Manuel joined Jordan in laughing at Ellie's remark. Ellie flopped back onto the rear seat and burped daintily. She excused herself and opened another beer.

Jordan turned in her seat. "Look to your left, Ellie. Pine trees are growing among those mangroves. Makes you feel kind of homesick, doesn't it? I'm surprised they can grow on such sandy loam."

"Yep. Home's great." Ellie agreed, before turning her attention to the cold beer in her hand. "If only cops back in Canada didn't get their panties in a twist about drinking and driving. What do you say about that, Jordan?"

Jordan ignored Ellie's effort to bait her into an argument as the vehicle geared down to swerve onto a narrow ledge. Manuel hit the brakes and killed the engine.

"Thought you'd like to take some pictures from this outlook." He gestured down to an amazing vista of turquoise waves caressing a pristine, white sandy shoreline.

"Great idea," Ellie said. Passing her third beer to Jordan, she stumbled from the back seat as she rummaged through her tote. "I know my camera's in here somewhere."

Jordan put her arm on Ellie's shoulder to steady her and help her step over a low railing to safeguard tourists

TARGETED   75

from tumbling over the edge of the cliff. "Shit!" Jordan circled several discarded condoms adorning the grassy bank. "This must be a popular parking spot."

"What can I say? We Hondurans are a friendly people," Manuel answered matter-of-factly in true guide fashion.

At last, Ellie extracted a compact digital camera from her bag. She clicked off several shots from their bird's-eye view. Jordan held onto the back of her cover up to make sure she didn't lose her footing.

Manuel saw the women approach a vendor encouraging tourists to have their picture taken sitting on a forlorn-looking donkey. He said, "We should hit the road now. I have much more to show you." Not waiting for their response, he jumped over the railing, rushed back, and held the passenger door open.

Ellie shoved her camera into her bag and extended her hand to Jordan. "I'll take my beer back now."

CHAPTER 20

Manuel's shirt crept up as he leaned to pull back the front passenger's seat for Ellie to climb in. A sheathed combat knife hung from the left side of his belt. Jordan's feeling of serenity dissolved like ice cream spilled on a hot sidewalk.

When Ellie was settled in, Jordan lifted one sandaled foot into the Jeep. Her heel bumped an object that had rolled from under the seat. A roll of gray duct tape. She recalled Tate's warning, and her senses sharpened. She still had time to leap out of the vehicle, but that would leave Ellie in Manuel's hands. She scanned the isolated road behind them, hoping to see another vehicle she could flag down.

Barely did she get her right foot pulled safely inside

before Manuel slammed the door and jumped into the driver's seat. Her mind struggled for an escape plan. She could no longer ignore the signs that screamed they had willingly placed themselves in a life-threatening situation.

As he swerved back onto the road and continued up the pass, she bent over and groaned, "I shouldn't have had that second cocktail on the beach. Take us back to Coxen Hole. I need a toilet. Now!"

"I'll pull over and you can squat behind those bushes on the other side of the road. I'll look the other way."

"Not good enough!" Jordan countered through clenched teeth. She leaned over and put her hand on the dash, grimacing in pain.

Ellie shot a puzzled glance her way. With a sigh, she dropped her empty can into the cooler and picked up a full one. Leaning forward, she prodded Jordan in the back. "What's up with you? You pee in the bushes lots of times at your parents' cottage."

Jordan turned her head and mouthed at Ellie, "Danger."

"Huh?" Ellie's befuddled mind finally registered the warning. "On second thought, a pee break is a great idea."

Manuel continued driving. "But you haven't seen the view from the top of the mountain range yet." His foot pressed down on the accelerator.

Jordan scowled as she forced another whimper past her lips. "Screw the view! Get me to a toilet fast unless you want a mess on this seat."

Manuel swore in Spanish. He slammed on the brakes and turned into a small clearing before wrenching the steering wheel to back out onto the road. The movement caused the sleeve on his right shoulder to inch up. Jordan caught a clear view of his tattoo—a blue dagger with red blood droplets falling onto the letters, *Madras 16*.

Shit and double shit.

CHAPTER 21

Manuel's abrupt change of mood on the harrowing descent down the mountain road was not lost on Jordan.

A dilapidated shack, with faded images of liquor bottles and food items, came into view.

She had hoped to see other vehicles parked there so she could ask someone for help. But they were the only visitors.

Propelling backward into the small parking spot, he slammed his foot on the brake. Jordan grabbed the dash to avoid a face plant.

Ellie whined, "Shit, man, take it easy. I nearly spilled my beer."

He left them to open their own door. Walking a few

yards away, he turned his back on them, mumbling, "I'll wait here and have a smoke."

Jordan flung her door open and jumped from the jeep. As Ellie crouched to follow, Jordan leaned close to her ear and whispered, "Bring your bag and hurry."

Propelling Ellie to the outhouse beside the cafe, Jordan opened the door and pushed her inside.

"Ouch! Don't be so rough. You know I bruise easily."

"Ellie, sober up and listen to me. Our guide's packing—"

"Yes, I noticed he has a nice package." Ellie smirked then belched.

Jordan grabbed Ellie by her upper arms and shook her hard, itching to slap her friend across the face. "Pay attention—our lives may depend on it! He has a concealed dagger, a roll of duct tape on the floor of the Jeep, and a tattoo with 'Madras 16' on his upper arm. I recognized the tattoo from last night's news. He's a gang member and some of his buddies were arrested for drug trafficking in La Ceiba."

Frustrated with the still vacant look in Ellie's eyes, Jordan gave her another shake before repeating, "La Ceiba. You know. The place where the airport bus let us off."

Ellie's liquor-fuelled high crashed and burned. "Holy shit. You got to be kidding!"

"Do I look like I'm kidding? Follow me."

Jordan risked a peek around the door to ensure Manuel wasn't watching. They sprinted twenty-five feet from

TARGETED 83

the outhouse and squatted behind a dense thicket of brush. From here, they could watch him.

Manual tossed his cigarette butt to the ground and stormed over to the outhouse door. Pounding with fisted hands, he yelled, "Ellie…Jordan…Get out here. We need to get going, now!"

When no response came, he swung the door open with such force that the top hinge dislodged. He stared at two empty stalls. A string of Spanish and English curses exploded from his mouth as he backed out and scanned the roadside. Jordan pushed Ellie's head down in case her bright hair betrayed their position.

Manuel raced to his Jeep, pulling his cell phone out. He fired up the engine and sped in the direction of the village while screaming into his phone.

Jordan and Ellie waited several minutes to make sure he was well away before jumping up and running for their lives.

CHAPTER 22

They struggled through jungle terrain, keeping the road in sight. When they heard a vehicle approaching, they dropped to the ground and waited until it passed. They could trust no one. If Manuel had called in other gang members, they would be forced to run deeper into the jungle. Ellie was tiring, and Jordan pulled her along, forging a path through the thick foliage.

The fear of spending the night in the jungle kept them pressing forward. It seemed hours before they rounded a bend and spotted the outlines of dusty buildings ahead. Staying low, they crept forward.

Jordan suppressed a curse of frustration—the decrepit Jeep was parked at the curb, and Manuel held binoculars to his eyes, searching the road in both directions. She clutched Ellie by the arm. "Quick, back into the bush!"

They hunkered back down until they heard the Jeep drive away.

Jordan pointed at a gaggle of tourists milling about the entrance to a small shack selling island rum. "Our best chance is to lose ourselves in that group so we can plan our next move."

They scurried across the road and mingled with the crowd. The tourists chattered in what sounded like German. Jordan fell in behind a tall couple, towing Ellie in her wake.

"Let's ask these people for help," Ellie whispered.

"Even if we can make ourselves understood, we might be putting their lives in danger, too."

The couple was oblivious to the women shadowing them. Jordan leaned around her German tourist and risked a glance into the street. The Jeep roared past the crowd, kicking up a dust storm.

She pushed down on her friend's head. "Stay low! The bastard is still searching for us and he looks pissed."

Jordan cursed herself for not buying an international calling package for her cell phone. She'd be able to call Tate for help, or perhaps even Darcy. Better yet, she longed for her police-issued Glock. She bobbed up again and dragged a distraught Ellie with her.

"Keep it together, Ellie."

Ellie began to cry in earnest so Jordan tried to calm her. "Listen. We'll find a taxi to take us back to our hotel."

TARGETED   87

They crossed the narrow street and followed a path between a maze of vendors displaying beaded necklaces, straw hats, and colorfully embroidered smocks. A block farther, they stumbled into a hat store to catch their breath and cool off in front of a floor fan emitting sounds like the death rattle of a water buffalo.

"Ellie, I'm going to tell you something. Promise you won't freak out on me."

"You mean you have worse news than we were nearly abducted as toys for a Honduran street gang and are, this minute, being hunted down like ducks in October? And, oh yeah, we happened to select a resort that already has a missing female guest."

"I get your point. But I didn't mention that I've seen cops on the dock arguing with Tate and on the second floor behind our unit with a sniffer dog. An ambulance left the back of the resort without lights or siren on. And, before I forget, Darcy told us he's on vacation, yet he's been meeting with an older cop, maybe the Chief. And I saw him break into Tate's office."

"You know, Jordan, sometimes your timing just plain sucks."

Jordan couldn't argue with that. "Just saying, I'm not sure we can trust anyone on this island."

CHAPTER 23

A gigantic punch bowl generously spiked with dark rum formed the main attraction at Happy Hour. Guests gyrated to melodies played by a four-piece steel band. Darcy chatted up Hannah, the blonde social convener from Australia, while keeping an eye on Robson.

As a young islander walked by with a tray of empty glasses, Robson reached out and spun him around. "Hold on there. Who are you, and why isn't José working his shift?"

"Oh, Señor Robson, José, he is very sick tonight. I'm his cousin, Pedro. I fill in for him."

Robson let go of his arm. "Very well, then. Make sure the punch bowl doesn't run dry."

"*Si, señor.*" The young man bobbed his head and rushed back behind the bar.

At a nod from her boss, Hannah snatched a limbo stick from behind the bar and held it up. She waved to the band leader, who shouted, "What time is it?"

The crowd yelled back, "It's limbo time!"

The band swung into the popular island song as guests formed a queue behind the limbo stick.

Darcy was first in line. He bent backward at his knees and, beer in hand, with slow, muscular foot movements, inched forward under the pole without spilling a drop. The crowd cheered as he straightened up and bowed before joining Robson at the bar.

The manager looked at his watch. "Have you seen Jordan and Ellie?"

"Not since this morning. Why?"

"They left at three-thirty p.m. with a local who offered to give them a tour of the island. Against my recommendation, I might add."

Taking another sip of his beer, Darcy said, "And your point is?"

"They said they'd be back before six."

"Relax, old boy. They'll probably pop up any minute now."

"The island is only thirty miles long," Robson stated tersely.

Darcy slammed his bottle down on the bar. "Get your keys. We're going to look for them."

TARGETED   91

"I'll meet you out front in ten minutes," Tate confirmed.

Darcy jogged up to his room to get his wallet and
change out of flip flops into runners. Before leaving, he
gathered up the papers spread across his bed, shoved them
into his briefcase, and locked it.

CHAPTER 24

Jordan, how could we have been sucked in by that little asshole? I shudder to think of what he and his gang buddies had in mind for us."

"We should have listened to Tate and not trusted a local," Jordan said through tight lips. And she should have heeded her own instincts.

Ellie was recovering. In fact, she appeared slightly cocky after their escape. "I hope that scumbag is laughed out of the gang when they find out we outwitted him."

Jordan noticed a beat up Crown Victoria pull to the curb across the road. A hand-written taxi sign was taped to the back side window. She grabbed Ellie's arm, checked for traffic and wandering goats, and steered her friend to the idling vehicle.

Ellie's expression brightened. "Sweet. We've missed Happy Hour but can salvage some of the evening."

Jordan leaned in the open passenger's window and addressed the female driver. "Are you available for a fare to Barefoot Bay resort?"

The young woman smiled and replied, "*Sí.*"

Jordan opened the back door and climbed in, sliding over to make room for Ellie.

The driver pulled the four-door sedan into a trickle of village traffic.

The exhausted women sank back into their seat to let the warm breeze from the open windows blow across their over-heated bodies.

Ellie lifted damp coils of hair from the nape of her neck and reached into her bag for their one remaining water bottle. She handed it to Jordan. "Nothing like running for your life to work up a thirst, eh, buddy?"

Jordan took a swig then passed it back, allowing her eyes to close. Immediately, they flew back open. She swiveled to face Ellie. "Don't mention this little episode to our families. They were worried enough when we told them we were vacationing in Honduras."

"Mum's the word." Ellie promised.

Jordan was resolved, however, to discuss their ordeal with one of the several police officers who were hanging about the resort.

എരഹ

Ellie covered a yawn as she looked out her window. "You know I'm directionally challenged, but I could have sworn that our hotel was back that way." She jerked her head to the west, a spastic motion that reminded Jordan of a bass trying to dislodge a hook.

Suddenly, the Crown Vic skidded to a stop beside a parked Dodge. Before they had time to react, their driver slid from the car. A man jumped behind the wheel and the vehicle took off. It thundered up the mountain pass leading to the remote eastern part of the island. The force of the acceleration threw the women into alternate corners of the back seat. As they struggled to right themselves, the power windows shot up, and the doors locked with an audible *click*.

A chorus of, "What the fuck!" catapulted from the back seat.

Dark, hooded eyes leered at them from the overhead mirror as if they were morsels to be sampled. A raspy voice barked, "Remember, me, José, your friendly bartender?" He removed his left hand from the steering wheel to lift the right sleeve of his stained tee shirt. Even with the metal grille between them, the gruesome tattoo glistened clearly on his sweaty bicep.

"Madras 16," he mocked. "Manuel is my baby brother. Our bros at the club house are waiting to party with you bitches." Both hands returned to the steering wheel to keep the heavy car from veering off the narrow road.

While Ellie was spewing obscenities at their captor,

Jordan's hands worked at the door lock on her side. It was a futile effort. With bruised fingers, she groped in her bag for a weapon. She had to find an object narrow and sharp enough to fit through the grille and pierce the monster's neck. Damn! She'd left her nail file at home to avoid problems with airport security. Withdrawing her hand, she heard the soft crinkling of the paper bag Tate had given them.

She forced her unsteady fingers to withdraw the contents. When she read the label on the can, adrenaline pumped through her body.

José swiveled his head to check out the noise just as Jordan shouted to Ellie, "Cover your eyes!" She lunged at the grill and pressed the button on the canister in her hand. "Take that, you bastard!"

A stream of liquid fire hit the driver's eyes. His screams mingled with Ellie's joyful, "Yesses!" as the pepper spray temporarily blinded him. Mucous ran from his nose to join the drool cascading from his gasping mouth.

The car careened from side to side then shuddered to a halt. A ham-sized fist pounded the buttons on the driver's door. The locks disengaged and José's hand found the handle. Opening the door, he dropped like a stone onto the road. A dust cloud billowed around him as he rolled and crawled away from the car.

Every few yards, he stopped to rub his damaged eyes. The soles of his sandaled feet disappeared into the mangroves, but still, they heard his spine-chilling cries of pain.

TARGETED   97

Jordan dropped the empty canister onto the floor. "Remind me to kiss Tate when we get back to the hotel. And I thought he had packed us bottled water."

The pepper spray residue caused them to wheeze and their eyes to smart. Jordan wiped her eyes with a handful of tissues from her bag and passed some to Ellie. "Quick, get into the front seat and put your window down to let fresh air in!"

The women hopped into the front seat of the idling car. Jordan performed a U-turn and started back down the mountain pass. They were running on pure adrenaline as they dabbed their inflamed eyes and laughed at the irony of driving to safety in the thug's car.

CHAPTER 25

As the Crown Vic rounded the first bend in the road, a vehicle screamed to a halt in front of them, blocking their descent. Manuel launched himself out, dagger in hand. His face, twisted in rage, showed no sign of his former boyish charm. "Get into my Jeep, bitches," he snarled.

The women froze. He opened the passenger side door and grabbed a handful of Ellie's hair, dragging her out of the car. "We don't want to keep my bros waiting, do we?"

He shoved Ellie against the side of his Jeep. Turning to Jordan, he hollered, "Don't even think of trying to get away or I'll stick your friend."

Manuel set the knife on the hood to open the passenger door. He reached under the front seat and pulled out the duct tape. Shoving Ellie face down on the seat, he wrenched her hands behind her back.

"Take it easy, asshole!" Ellie screamed. Ignoring her, he bound her wrists with the tape then crouched and did the same to her ankles.

Jordan stepped purposefully away from the Crown Vic. While he was distracted with Ellie's squirming body, she edged closer to the knife on the Jeep's hood. Manuel caught her movement out of the corner of his eye and snatched it up, sneering at her. He pulled Ellie back up and shoved her onto the back seat like a bag of sugar cane.

Landing face down, Ellie turned her head and screamed, "Run. Get help!"

Jordan sprinted toward the mangrove copse, hoping to draw him away from Ellie. It worked. His pounding footsteps closed the gap. Jacked on adrenaline, she stopped, and whirled to face her opponent.

Manuel advanced, duct tape clutched in one hand, the dagger in the other. He leaped at her, raising the dagger, poised to strike. She sidestepped and aimed a high kick at him. He threw his body aside at the last second, and her foot glanced off his shoulder. His eyes narrowed in surprise, and he dropped the duct tape. One hand was now free.

"Glad that got your attention, asshole," she jeered. "Not so cocksure of yourself now, are you?"

Repositioning herself, Jordan feigned a right jab to his kidney with her fist but kneed him in the crotch instead.

TARGETED   101

As he doubled over, she slammed him on the bridge of the nose with the hard ridge of her right palm. She skipped away as blood from his broken nose cascaded down his face. He dropped to the ground.

"Yo, bitch! Still want to party with us?" Jordan goaded.

Fury fueled her actions. She stomped on his right hand and bent to yank the dagger from his fingers.

Manuel clutched his balls and rolled into a fetal position, whimpering. Jordan kicked him on the side of the head, just because it felt so damn good. Her only regret was that she wasn't wearing her service boots.

Leaning down, inches from his distorted face, Jordan asked between gritted teeth, "How are you liking me, now, princess?"

Manuel gave a guttural groan.

She started back to the Jeep to free Ellie, but the roar of an oncoming vehicle stopped her in her tracks.

José or Manuel had had plenty of time to call in more gang members. Dagger in position, she took a stand and waited.

CHAPTER 26

Tate hit the brakes. Darcy shot him a dirty look as he grabbed the "holy shit" bar inside the SUV. When the dust cleared, he had to blink several times to comprehend what his eyes were telling him.

Jordan stood at the side of the road in a fighter's stance. She clutched a knife close to her hip, the blade pointing upward. Splatters of blood and dirt streaked her face and arms. Her chest heaved as she glared at them from behind a tangle of matted hair.

She looked magnificent. Darcy would remember this sight forever.

They burst from the vehicle. As recognition dawned, Jordan relaxed her knife arm. The men rushed past her to restrain Manuel who was trying to get to his feet.

Tate waved a Taser at Manuel. "Go ahead, dickhead. I'll make you dance like a ballerina."

Glowering at the newcomers, the youth fell back on his rump.

Darcy picked up the duct tape that lay on the road. "Bloody well done, Robson. For coming prepared, that is. Taser him and let's see if he pisses himself."

"I will if he moves a muscle," Tate promised. "Tape him up."

"My pleasure."

Darcy planted his foot on Manuel's back and shoved him back down onto the road. He grabbed the cursing thug and wrapped his hands behind his back, then secured his ankles. With Manuel hogtied, he sauntered over to Jordan. He turned her around and gave her a hard kiss on the lips as he removed the dagger from her hand. "Need to borrow your knife, love, but gotta say. You're amazing."

Jordan half-heartedly shoved him away and hung onto the Jeep to keep her balance.

Darcy spoke soothingly to Ellie. "Hold on, little one. I'll have you free in a sec." He cut through the tape binding her, helped her to an upright position, and eased her out of the vehicle. He handed the dagger to Jordan. "Hang on to this, but lose it before going back through airport security."

They watched Tate drag Manuel by the collar and toss him in the back of the Suburban. Slamming the door, he said, "The bastard can cook in there until the police arrive.

I saw his 'Madras 16' tat." He approached Jordan, "Are you hurt?"

"Just my pride, Tate, and my foot's a little tender. I kicked the asshole a few times, and these sandals didn't cushion the impact worth a damn."

"You're alive. That's all that matters." He turned to Ellie. "How about you? Are you injured?"

Ellie stopped hugging Darcy long enough to answer in a nasal tone. "My nose got smushed into the filthy back seat, and my wrists hurt. And I'll likely need to see a shrink when I get back home after two kidnapping attempts in one day."

"Two?" Darcy repeated, trying to make sense of her remark.

Jordan sighed deeply. "Yes, two. When I saw our bogus tour guide's gang tattoo and knife, we managed to escape. Unfortunately, he called his brother, José, for backup. He sucked us in by using one of their women as a taxi driver. They traded places before we knew what was happening."

"José's a gang member, too?" Tate asked in astonishment. "That explains why he wasn't at work today."

"Yes." Jordan flexed her stiffening right hand. "We really screwed up by not taking your advice in the first place." She gave Ellie a pointed look as she limped over to lean against the Suburban.

Tate handed the Taser to Darcy. "Hold this while I call the police."

"I always wanted one of these. Maybe I'll order one off e-Bay." Darcy grinned like a kid at Christmas as he examined the weapon. He was inordinately pleased to see Jordan smile and shake her head at his remark.

CHAPTER 27

After Tate told the police where to find them, Jordan gave him a hug. "Thanks for slipping the pepper spray to us. José can verify how well it worked."

"It was a last resort when I couldn't talk you out of going on a tour with a local."

"Oh, I almost forgot. José is crawling around in the bushes back there." She pointed over her shoulder with her thumb.

"You are a woman to be reckoned with, aren't you, love?" Darcy said. "I may have to steal you away from the Toronto Police Service."

Jordan let the remark slide. He better not be offering her a job at his Hooters Bar.

"Piermont, let's go collect my former employee." Looking down at the roll in Darcy's hand, Tate said, "Damn, I see we're short on duct tape."

"No worries." Darcy bent down and took the thick laces out of his runners. "These should do."

Tate slapped Darcy on the back, harder than strictly necessary. "I'll bet you were a boy scout when you were a kid."

"Actually, no, I'm not into roughing it. But I've collected some interesting tips from shady bar patrons during my travels."

"The keys are in the ignition," Tate said to the women. "Climb in and crank up the air. If anyone other than the police show up, sound the horn. As soon as we round up José, we'll turn these scumbags over and take you back to the resort."

Darcy handed the Taser to Jordan. "I'm sure you know how this works if you need to use it."

"I do," Jordan said. "And, Tate, thanks for not saying 'I told you so.'"

"We all make mistakes. And, besides, you had things under control by the time we showed up."

Darcy tired of listening to Tate's big hero act and set off to retrieve José. Tate caught up to him and they followed a wide swathe of crushed ferns. They found José propped against a palm tree, rubbing his reddened eyes. Hearing footsteps, he tried to crawl away but was stopped by Darcy's foot to the back of his neck.

TARGETED 109

"Just go with the wrist restraints," Tate suggested. "We don't want to drag his heavy ass back to the SUV."

They each grabbed a bicep to hoist José to his feet.

"Nice tat, fuckhead," Darcy commented as he tightened his grip. "Your buddies will piss themselves laughing when word spreads you were beaten up by a woman."

Prying José's hands from his eyes, he roughly bound them behind his back with the shoe laces. After patting the thug down, Darcy dropped a switchblade and a set of brass knuckles into the deep pockets of his cargo shorts.

They shoved José forward as a police van rumbled to a stop. "I almost forgot," Tate said. "Consider yourself off the payroll."

A uniformed cop took charge of José, while two more dragged a struggling Manuel out of the back of the Suburban. They threw the brothers into the police van.

After locking the door of the van, an officer approached Robson, notepad in hand. "We'll need a statement from the *señoritas*."

"Understood, but they've been through a terrible ordeal. They're tourists staying at my resort. I'm taking them back there now. Drop by my office in the morning, say at ten a.m., and they'll give you statements then."

The young officer gave a curt nod before climbing into the driver's side of the van and taking off like a rocket. Darcy felt a moment of elation as he envisioned Manuel's and José's restrained bodies ricocheting around in the back of the vehicle on the hair-pin curves heading to jail.

CHAPTER 28

Tate hurried to his office, saying he had pressing business that required his attention. Darcy accompanied Jordan and Ellie to their room.

The women invited Darcy in and collapsed on their beds.

"I'm getting lightheaded from low blood sugar," Jordan said.

"I'll order dinner," Darcy offered. "Here's an appetizer." He tossed both women a banana from the bowl.

Jordan peeled hers and took a bite, wishing it was hamburger and French fries. With gravy. "By the way, our water pressure is good now. Yours should be, too."

He dropped into one of the easy chairs. "Did Robson ever say what caused the problem?"

"No, we can ask him that tomorrow. Tonight, I'm not moving out of this room." Jordan looked over at Ellie. "And, neither are you."

"I wouldn't quiz him about a plumbing repair. I'm sure he has more important concerns to deal with," Darcy said.

He got up and squeezed himself down beside Jordan before picking up the phone. He spoke in Spanish to order their meals from room service. "Ellie, I'll entertain Jordan while you shower. It will be at least twenty minutes before our food arrives."

Ellie rolled painfully off her bed and pulled an outfit from her dresser drawer.

After the bathroom door closed, Jordan gave him a shove. "Move over! What's your problem?"

He hesitated, not sure which problem she was talking about.

"You're holding back on me. Spit it out! Why did you have a meeting with a cop in your room? And why did you break into Tate's office in the middle of the night?"

"You're good, Jordan. I was unaware I was being watched, either time."

"And I don't believe you're here on vacation. Tell me what you're up to, or I go to Tate for answers."

"Now that would be a dangerous move."

The shower stopped running.

He lowered his voice. "Wait until Ellie's asleep and come to my room. I'll explain what I can then."

TARGETED 113

Jordan eyed him suspiciously then leaned over and whispered, "I'll think about it."

Ellie, in her red newly-purchased tee shirt, joined them just as the food arrived. While they devoured their late meal, Ellie filled him in on the two abduction attempts. By the time she was done, he wanted to chew his own ears off to stop her endless chatter. He'd rather have had the Coles Notes version from Jordan. He escaped to his room around midnight.

❧❧❧

Darcy spent most of what remained of the night tossing and turning and unwinding the sheets that threatened to strangle him. He listened for a soft tap on his door that never came. Just before dawn, he lost the battle to stay awake and fell into a deep sleep.

CHAPTER 29

Jordan pried her eyes open, glanced at the clock, then jumped out of bed and shook Ellie awake. They bolted down their room-service breakfast before heading to Tate's office for their ten a.m. interview with the police.

Jordan felt a shred of guilt that she hadn't gone to Darcy's room last night. But after he left, she had been too physically exhausted and emotionally tapped out to do anything except fall into bed.

She resolved to pump him for information after the police interview.

⋐⋑⋐⋑

They hesitated when they got off the elevator and saw

Darcy in the doorway of Tate's office. He left without seeing them. Jordan knocked on the closed door.

"*Introduzca.*"

A uniformed officer sat at Tate's desk. Jordan recognized him as the cop who had entered Darcy's suite with the laundry cart.

"Please have a seat, *Señoritas*. Thank you for coming to give your statements. I am Chief Florés."

"I'm Jordan Blair and this is Ellie Cassidy." They sat on the visitors' chairs.

"It's a pleasure to meet you both, although I wish it were under different circumstances," Florés said. He inclined his head at Jordan. "I am especially pleased to meet a fellow officer from Canada."

"Thank you. The pleasure is mine."

"Why isn't Tate here? He's the one who came to our rescue and set up our appointment with you," Ellie asked.

"I'm afraid I have some unpleasant news to tell you. Darcy Piermont tells me that you are aware of the disappearance of Maryanne Reston."

They nodded in unison.

"Her body has been found. The results of the autopsy have determined that Ms. Reston was murdered."

"Shut up! I mean, no way," Ellie blurted, before clapping a hand over her mouth.

"She was hit over the head with a heavy, pointed object and suffered an immediate and fatal brain bleed. And you two, inadvertently, helped us locate her body."

Jordan and Ellie shared a bewildered look. He continued. "My officers were called when a maintenance worker found the cause of the water pressure problem that you reported." He paused to give the women time to digest what he was saying. "Ms. Reston's body was floating in the resort's water tank and had settled in front of the filter."

The color drained from Ellie's face. Jordan grabbed the back of her neck and forced her head down lower than her body.

Chief Florés jumped up and poured a glass of water. He handed it to Ellie when her head bobbed back up. She took a large gulp and smiled a weak thanks. Turning slowly to Jordan, she said in a shaky whisper, "We were showering in that water."

"Try not to think about that," Jordan encouraged as she patted Ellie's knee. But her stomach did a series of rapid flips. She turned to the chief. "Have you caught her murderer?"

"Not yet, but we have a suspect with a strong motive, thanks to the expertise of the private investigator on loan to us."

"Can you tell us who you suspect so we can be sure to avoid him or her?" Jordan asked. Icy worms of dread shinnied up her veins as she waited for his response.

"Sorry. I can't discuss an open investigation. Before I forget, Señor Piermont asked me to invite you to join him at the pool bar when you're done here."

"Okay, but that doesn't explain why Tate isn't here." Ellie's face had regained some color and her voice sounded less like a frightened child's.

"We're not sure where he is, but that's not your concern. Now, back to the reason you *are* here." He slid forms and pens across the desk. "Take your time and write down all details about the attempted abductions by the 'Madras 16' gang members, Manuel and José Playla."

"Their mother must be so proud," Jordan commented before starting to write.

Staring at the blank sheet in front of her, Ellie asked apprehensively, "Does it have to be in essay form?"

A smile made its way through Florés' luxurious, salt and pepper moustache, "Point form is fine, my dear."

CHAPTER 30

Walking along the pathway to the bar, Ellie sighed with relief. "Well, that was an ordeal, wasn't it?"

"Yep. Even I need a drink now," Jordan confessed. "It must be five o'clock somewhere."

"I can't believe I'm saying this, but I'm going to order virgin drinks for the rest of our stay. I need to keep my wits about me." Ellie looked sad, but determined.

They saw Darcy sitting alone at a table drawing figure eights on the glass top with the moisture from his beer bottle.

He looked unusually solemn but forced a smile when he saw them. "I hope Florés wasn't too hard on you."

"It wasn't pleasant, but it's worth it if it keeps those two animals behind bars," Jordan said as they sat down.

"It was far worse hearing that the woman who had stayed in our room was found dead, floating in the water tank," Ellie said in an octave higher than normal.

"Yes, that was very tragic." Darcy gave Ellie's shoulders a light squeeze before continuing. "The chief has given me permission to confide in you. I'm not here on vacation. I was hired by the resort's board of directors to investigate Maryanne Reston's disappearance."

"So you're the private investigator the chief told us about." Pieces of the puzzle started to fall into place for Jordan. "And why would the hotel chain hire you? Isn't this a local police matter?"

"Normally, yes, but the resort owners are clients of mine. They asked me to get involved because they suspected a—well, an inside job, frankly."

"That's your third business!" Ellie exclaimed, looking at Darcy with admiration. You'd think she had just seen white smoke rising from the Vatican chimney.

"Piermont Investigations. Head Office in Montreal, with branch offices in London and Madrid. My grandfather started the firm in 1967.

"Then you know who the murder suspect is." Jordan folded her arms and gave Darcy an insistent stare. She was sick of his evasive comments.

"Unfortunately, yes."

Ellie put her hand up to stop him from continuing. She

waved the waiter over and ordered a beer for Jordan and orange juice for herself.

Darcy waited until their drinks had been delivered. "The resort owners suspected fraudulent use of funds. They sent one of their chartered accountants, Maryanne Reston, to investigate. She met with Robson on two occasions and emailed a report to head office. It stated that there were discrepancies in the resort's books. She suspected Robson was implicated. Her next step would have been to demand access to his private accounts. When Maryanne failed to contact head office on her third day here, they reported her missing."

He looked at Jordan's troubled expression, then down at his beer before continuing. "I discovered Robson has a gambling addiction and has racked up serious debts to some very unsavory characters."

"Not Tate!" Ellie wailed. "I don't believe you."

"Easy now, *chérie*. I know this is upsetting news, but you need to know what has transpired here—for your own protection. I trust you will keep this information to yourselves until the investigation is concluded."

Both women nodded as they picked up their drinks from the table.

"The autopsy was fast tracked, and it showed that Maryanne was hit on the back of the head with a heavy object with a sharp point."

"Chief Florés told us," Ellie said and made a face.

Jordan wasn't sure if her grimace was from the details

of the murder or the lack of vodka in her orange juice.

"I visited Tate's office in the wee hours of yesterday and noticed that the award, shaped like a Macaw, could be the murder weapon." Glancing back at Jordan, he continued. "While Robson and I were looking for you yesterday, the chief's forensic team tested the statue for blood residue."

Jordan forced herself to ask. "And it tested positive?"

"Correct." Darcy leaned back in his chair. "It had been wiped clean of fingerprints—except for a partial thumb print on the bottom. Belonging to Robson."

Jordan winced as she remembered reaching over to touch the award. Lucky for her, Tate had pulled her away from it.

Darcy saw that her mind had wandered and touched her hand to regain her attention. "We suspect that when Maryanne confronted Robson, he panicked, hit her over the head, and hid her body until he could figure out how to dispose of it."

"That's why Florés visited your room with the laundry cart. Tate used the cart to transport her body to the water reservoir," Jordan said with resignation.

"There's a door close to your room. It leads to the storage tank. And, yes, we found Maryanne's blood inside the cart." In an effort to lighten the mood around the table, Darcy said, "Jordan, you really should consider putting your talents to use working for me."

"Slow down there, Skippy," Jordan replied. "I have a

TARGETED 123

job." She was grateful that this job offer wouldn't require dancing on tables.

"I can't see Tate as a killer," Ellie said, "There must be another explanation."

"For what it's worth, I'm sure he didn't plan to murder Maryanne. He must have felt trapped and reacted on impulse."

"Where is he now?" Jordan asked.

"He's a smart fellow. I'm guessing he's lost himself on one of the Caribbean islands and will never be apprehended. There will be a warrant out for his arrest, so he won't be able to return to Honduras or Canada. A replacement manager is flying in tomorrow."

Jordan drained the last of her beer and rose from her chair. "Will you excuse us, Darcy? Ellie and I need to go to our room and decide whether to stick out the rest of the week, or fly back home as soon as we can get a flight out. Come on, Ellie."

"I hope you decide to stay," Darcy called after them. "I promise to stick close by you."

"I'm not sure if that makes me feel better or worse," Jordan muttered to Ellie as they entered the lobby.

CHAPTER 31

They decided to cut their vacation short by three days. Jordan called the airline to book their flights home for the following day.

Determined to enjoy their last day in the sun, they pulled on swimsuits and went down to the pool area. Over coffee and banana bread, Ellie insisted on discussing men, deceitful men to be specific. She declared she would never trust another man as long as she lived. They had mistakenly trusted three dangerous men already.

Jordan let Ellie vent before reminding her about Darcy's initial warning. Honduras had the highest crime rate per capita in the world.

Did they heed his warning? Nope, and look where that got them—targeted by a vicious gang.

"Maybe, he should have added—beware of hot resort managers, too," Ellie said with a catch in her voice.

"Let's not forget that Tate saved us by giving us the pepper spray. Most criminals have some redeeming qualities."

Jordan looked up and saw Darcy flip-flopping across the cement pool deck.

"Aha! Here you are, my beauties." Darcy pulled a chair over and sat down. "You're both looking more chipper today. I was afraid you had left without even saying goodbye."

Jordan hitched her chair away to give him more room. "Morning, Darcy. We've had enough of Caribbean magic but our flight doesn't leave until tomorrow."

"Can't say that I blame you."

"Have you been up to anything exciting this morning?" Ellie asked.

"I've been hanging out in Robson's office with Florés. I'm afraid people will start thinking we're a couple," Darcy said, with a wink.

"Any sign of Tate?" Ellie asked. "I still hope he can explain his actions."

"Nope. Florés is checking with the ferry captains. He may have hired or stolen a boat to get to the mainland."

"Is your work here done now?" Jordan asked.

"Just about. I figure I might as well fly home tomorrow as well."

Jordan stood up. "We better get to our room and pack.

TARGETED 127

Are you free to dine with us on our last evening in paradise?"

"Nothing would please me more. We'll have one final pig-out at the buffet table. I promise to avoid the prawns."

CHAPTER 32

Except for last minute items, their packing was soon complete.

"I'm feeling restless, and I don't want to leave without snorkeling at the Roatán Marine Park," Jordan said. "Let's book a catamaran excursion through Hannah."

The social director informed them that a catamaran was leaving at one p.m. It would take them to a reef for an hour and then to the mainland. From there, they would board a bus for a one-hour sight-seeing tour along the coast.

They booked the excursion and made it to the dock with ten minutes to spare.

Jordan tried rotating her shoulders and rubbing her neck to release her knotted muscles. With Manuel and José locked up and Tate long gone, she wondered why she still felt tense.

❦❦❦

After his meeting with Florés, Darcy noticed Jordan's and Ellie's names on the excursion roster in the foyer. He signed himself up and hurried to join them.

About to ascend the steps to the dock, he saw a tall, hooded figure boarding behind the line of passengers. The man turned his head and Darcy caught a glimpse of his face. With a spurt of energy, he ran toward the catamaran. The boarding plank was hauled in before he reached it and the idling motor surged into forward gear. Not wanting to alarm the passengers by shouting at the crew, he hurried back to the hotel as the boat sailed out the mouth of the causeway. Bursting into the manager's office, he leaned on the desk puffing. The chief looked up and asked pleasantly, "Forget something, my friend?"

"I saw Robson board the catamaran that just left the dock. We have to stop him before he reaches the mainland and disappears. Jordan and Ellie are on board."

Florés retrieved the boat keys from his pocket. "Let's go. I'll alert my men."

Minutes later, Darcy jumped into the police boat as Florés bellowed, "Catch that catamaran."

❦❦❦

TARGETED 131

As the distance narrowed between the police craft and their target, Darcy's fingers clutched the side of the bucking boat. He scanned the occupants, desperate to locate Jordan and Ellie.

Then he spotted them. They were enjoying the ocean view, unaware that Robson was standing directly behind them.

Darcy clutched at the chief's arm and pointed. Florés shook him off. "I see him!"

When the catamaran was thirty feet away, Florés picked up a bullhorn and ordered the skipper to cut the engine and prepare to be boarded. The vessel came to a standstill as passengers voiced their concern.

The two younger officers scurried up the ladder onto the deck. It took Florés slightly longer to hoist his body aboard. Darcy frantically waited his turn. He landed inside to see Robson reach an arm around Ellie's neck, pulling her back against him.

CHAPTER 33

As Tate pressed a gun to the side of Ellie's head, Jordan recognized the desperation in his eyes. He bent his head and whispered, "Sorry, Ellie, but they're leaving me no choice."

"Tate, let me go!" Ellie pleaded.

He hung on. Ellie's body was a shield against the three police guns aimed at him. The other passengers scattered.

Jordan remained. She remembered Manuel's dagger and slid her hand inside her tote. Her movement caught Tate's attention.

"Jordan, don't even think of trying anything. Please."

Jordan slowly withdrew her hand but stood her ground.

"Put your weapons away, Florés. Don't force my hand!" Tate yelled.

"Don't be a fool, Robson. I've radioed my counterparts on the mainland. You have no place to run."

"You forget that I'm a gambler and have nothing to lose." Tate moved left several steps, dragging Ellie with him. The police adjusted their aims. "Florés, toss me the key to your boat, now!" Tate ordered.

"That is not going to happen, Robson."

Jordan prayed one of the cops wouldn't get trigger happy and shoot Ellie by mistake. She inched closer to Tate's gun arm.

In an effort to distract him, Darcy pleaded. "Come on, man. As a gambler, you know it's time to fold." Tate didn't respond so he continued on in a calm voice. "There are two ways you can get off this boat. The easy way is by putting down your gun and surrendering. Or in a body bag. Make the right choice, my friend."

When Tate's frantic eyes shifted from Darcy to the officers, a cold blast of certainty enveloped Jordan. Somebody was going to die today, and she didn't want it to be Ellie. Or Darcy.

She launched herself at Tate's gun arm, knocking it away from Ellie. Jordan placed both thumbs on top of his elbow, her fingers at the back, and dug into the nerve center, squeezing with all her strength.

Tate roared in pain and the gun dropped to the deck from his numb fingers. Jordan quickly kicked the weapon away. She forced Tate's temporarily useless arm behind him and upward to his shoulder blades. He released Ellie and dropped to his knees moaning. One of Florés men ran over and clamped on handcuffs.

Cheers from relieved passengers signaled the end of the takedown. Darcy helped Ellie up and then turned and gave Jordan a bear hug. "Remind me never to get on your bad side, my sweet."

As Tate was being loaded into the police boat, he called back to Darcy. "I didn't plan to kill her. Do me a favor? Start the paperwork on my extradition to a Canadian jail and get someone to deliver my meals."

A sliver of pity softened Darcy's expression. "You got it. Give the Playla brothers the finger for me."

The sudden release of tension left Jordan lightheaded. She moved closer to Darcy and allowed him to take her hand.

"Skipper, take these people back to the resort," the chief called out. "We'll need statements." He turned to Darcy. "And, Piermont, I'll meet you at the resort office after I deliver Robson to his jail cell. I'm sure your employer will be anxious for my report."

Florés inclined his head in Jordan's direction before following his men to their boat.

CHAPTER 34

I hereby pronounce this vacation nightmare officially over," Ellie declared, as they waited at the Juan Manuel Gálvez International Airport. "I don't even have a tan to show for all the money I spent."

Realizing neither Jordan nor Darcy were paying any attention to her complaints, she wandered over to the gift shop to buy some magazines.

Their flight would get them into Toronto at midnight EST. Darcy's flight to Montreal left two hours later than theirs, but he had insisted on accompanying them to the airport.

"I'm sorry your vacation was a disaster, Jordan. Given any thought to trying again next winter?"

"Not a chance! I can't shake the image of Tate holding a gun to Ellie's head. Between that and having to escape from gang thugs, twice, my love affair with Honduras is over."

"Montreal is beautiful in the fall. Why don't you come visit me for a few days?"

Jordan turned to him. This afternoon, he wore a navy tee shirt with the words, *Pissing off the Whole Planet, One Person at a Time*, emblazoned across the front. She was beginning to find his unique personality and fashion statements oddly amusing. She was even getting used to the crested hair that made him look like a blond cockatoo.

"You're probably seldom in your Montreal office," she countered.

He leaned over and slung his arm around her shoulder. "I have a secret, *chérie*. I'm in Montreal most of the time because my corporate office is there. Did you think I ran my businesses from the back room of a tattoo parlor? *Mais, non.*"

"Actually, I haven't given it much thought," Jordan admitted.

"My uncle runs the London office, and my Mom looks after the Madrid end of the business.

"So let me get this straight. You don't have a Hooters bar in Madrid or a tattoo parlor in Montreal?"

"I was pulling your leg with the Hooters thing. But, I do have an interest in a tattoo supply business in Montreal."

"I see," was all she could think of to say. Then a disembodied voice announced Flight 486 was now boarding. "That's us, Darcy." She waved frantically at Ellie who hustled over to join them.

Darcy refused to release her without an answer to his invitation. He slipped his business card into her pocket.

"Okay, we have a tentative plan," Jordan said as she tried to extricate herself. "You can let go now, Darcy. Geez, this is a public airport."

Ellie joined them and broke into a big grin. "You two should get a room. Give her a good one to remember you by, Darcy."

"Thank you, sweetie. I believe I will."

When their lips met, to Jordan's surprise, the throng of people milling about them seemed to vanish. She threw her arms around his neck and deepened their kiss.

℘℘℘

Their jet sped off the runway and climbed sharply, circling over La Ceiba Beach. Gazing down from her window seat, Jordan watched with amusement as tourists exited the buses. They resembled busy little ants, rushing in all directions. She was far too high to notice the leaves of the red ginger bush rustle in the motionless air.

About the Authors

Donna Warner

Donna Warner's career experiences prior to writing fiction include teaching adult education courses, owning a private vocational school, being a communication manager of a national toxicology research network, and working as a freelance editor. When not attempting to outsmart fish at her cottage, home is a country property near Guelph, Ontario, Canada. She enjoys tutoring English-as-a-second-language students and networking with fellow authors through social media and memberships in the International Thriller Writers (ITW) and the Crime Writers of Canada.

Gloria Ferris

A former technical writer, Gloria Ferris is the award-winning author of humorous mysteries *Cheat the Hangman* and *Corpse Flower*. *Targeted* is her first co-written suspense venture with author Donna Warner. When not writing, Ferris works on character profiles, researches plotlines, reads continuously, and is often heard to mutter, "I wish I'd written that!" She is a member of the Crime Writers of Canada, the Crime Writers' Association (UK), and the International Thriller Writers. She lives in southwestern Ontario.

CPSIA information can be obtained
at www.ICGtesting.com
Printed in the USA
LVOW04s0612281115
464483LV00032B/357/P